I0669003

Chance Meeting

by

Christine Columbus

The Wild Rose Press, Inc.
PO Box 708
Adams Basin, NY 14410-0708
Visit us at www.thewildrosepress.com

Publishing History
First Edition, 2025
Trade Paperback ISBN 978-1-5092-5969-4
Digital ISBN 978-1-5092-5970-0

Published in the United States of America

Dedication

Without help from my husband Rich, sister Colleen, sister-in-law Patty, friends, Pam and Anita, TWRP, Rhonda, RJ, and Leanne, this book would still be only be a word document on my computer. Thank you all for breathing life into Chance Meeting and giving me a chance to share my words with others.

Praise Comments

for CHANCE MEETING

"I think the readers will find Mel very relatable. Who hasn't felt, when it comes to life's decisions, that it seems like everyone else's welfare and happiness comes first. Through heartfelt and clever dialogue, you follow along as Mel comes to the realization that she needs to take responsibility for her own happiness before it's too late."

~Colleen R.

~*~

"I thoroughly loved the story. A good writer allows you to envision each character even without ever seeing them and I hated saying goodbye to them at the end of the book."

~Patricia F.

~*~

"I loved *Chance Meeting.*"

~Amanda F.

Chapter One

Melody Anderson sped past the *Welcome to Northeast Minneapolis* sign and didn't slow until she found a parking space at the back of Gascon's employee parking lot. She shouldered the worn laptop bag, grabbed her latte, and rushed toward the historic four-story, red brick building.

Ignoring the loud chorus of red-bellied robins and the fragrant lilacs, she continued her march to the employee entrance. The heel of her sandal caught. She lurched forward. The cup's lid popped off like a pilot ejected from an airplane as the computer bag shifted, and the steamy latte splashed onto the right sleeve of her summer sweater.

With scowl lines etched onto her forehead she yanked open the glass doors and entered the brightly lit lobby with the vacant receptionist's desk. Technology had replaced the friendly Mrs. Hobbs with a key fob. Now, no one greeted Melody in the morning or asked about her day. *Who's next?* Mel sneered at the sterile, impersonal space and shuffled to the antiquated elevator. She jabbed the down arrow. The elevator groaned, but the doors stayed closed. *Great.* She stomped through the door and clambered down the musty stairs to the basement.

She strode into her temporary office and flung the computer bag onto Bill's desk. A stack of papers toppled to the floor. "Sheesh!" She stormed down the battleship-gray hallway to the ladies' room and reappeared with fragments of white paper toweling clinging to her sleeve.

Tap. Tap-tap. Tap-tap…

What's next? Melody paused outside her office, tilting her head toward the sound.

Paula, her administrative assistant, jogged over the pewter vinyl tiles in lime-green, high-heeled sandals. She wore a faded and frayed denim skirt under an oversized man's white dress shirt. "You just missed him."

"*Humph,*" Melody sighed, glancing past the queen of chic's messy blonde bun and down the long, tiled hallway. "I'm not seeing anyone." She shrugged and stepped back into her temporary office.

"Did you not hear me say the word *missed*?" Paula tap-danced into the office. "A tall, dark-haired, brown-eyed man, without a wedding ring, was here."

Melody scanned the mess on the floor. "Just my luck. Mr. Right shows up, and I'm in the bathroom."

"Memos for floor covering? I don't think you'll be starting any trends." She teased. "You really should have refused the request from upper management. You already have too much on your…" Shrugging, she smiled. "I was going to say desk, but you solved that problem. But the good news is he did mention he'd be back."

She turned toward Paula. "Did he mention who he was?"

"General Manager of Construction Dunn Wright. You know, the company Bill hired for the office remodeling." Paula raised an eyebrow. "Mr. Good-

Looking wanted to go over some changes."

"What?" Melody tossed her hands up. "Could the day get any worse? I'm wearing unbecoming jeans and a wet, clingy coffee-stained sweater, and I might have forgotten to comb my hair."

"You don't look too bad." She cocked her head to the side. "Just run your fingers through your hair and pinch your cheeks for some color. Rough morning with Kansas?"

"In two months, when her mom comes home, I will miss these hectic mornings, but living with a six-year-old is work. We were running late. When I found Kansas, she was cleaning the bathroom floor with my electric toothbrush."

"Sorry." Paula smirked. "I'll make sure all of Bill's meetings show up in your calendar." She paused in the doorway. "Anything else?"

Melody shook her head and waited a moment before letting out a long sigh. *Mr. Good-looking. Chance and romance. When will Paula learn happily ever after is only for books?* In the center of the office, she stood glaring at the files overflowing from the cabinets, the blinking desk phone, and three computer monitors. "I should have said *no* to Leo's request to manage Bill's meetings and emails for two weeks."

Another mess to clean up. Squinting, she sighed. *What are my odds of encountering something sticky or creepy crawly?* Swallowing her reservations and discomfort, she dropped to her hands and knees and crawled slowly under the workstation. Gathering the last document, she heard an unfamiliar voice echoing outside the door.

"Is Melody back yet?"

She gazed beneath the desk. Work boots stood on the threshold of Bill's office. She stopped breathing as her gaze traveled higher to a pair of denim jeans. She tensed. *The general manager?* She inhaled through her nose. *Please go away.*

Tap-tap-tap.

Paula's glow-in-the-dark, high-heeled sandals and spray-tanned legs moved next to the boots and jeans.

"She was in her office a moment ago," Paula said.

Would I rather be a frazzled woman in a coffee-stained sweater or a person who is impossible to get a hold of? Mel sucked on her bottom lip and debated the options. A sharp, hot pain shot down her left calf and seized her thoughts. "Cramp," she mumbled with a backward, one-legged crawl. "Just so you know, you're not meeting me at my best."

A deep chuckle filled the room.

"What are you doing?" Paula shrieked.

Melody didn't stop crawling until her head cleared the desk. She stood with as much grace as a toddler with an armful of toys. She met his gaze. *Paula is right. He is handsome.* She blew a blonde strand of hair from her eyes.

He held out a hand. "Hello, Clayton Westby. And you must be Melody Anderson."

She dropped the mess of papers onto the desk. "Yes." She stretched her right arm out.

His eyebrows drew together, and his gaze narrowed as his warm hand encased hers. "Have we met before?"

"No," Melody blurted. "I am certain I would have remembered you."

He shrugged and leisurely released her hand.

"Well, nice to meet you. Bill mentioned you would be helping him out for a couple of weeks. I have a few changes for the remodeling project."

"Bill assured me he had given you all the details." She shifted her attention to the stack of papers on the desk. "I'm not sure I can help."

"You just need to approve a few minor changes." Clayton held up a cylinder in his left hand. "If I could show you some options, and see what you think?"

"Conference room three is booked." Paula winked. "Would anyone like coffee?"

"Please." Melody smoothed her damp sleeve while she followed him down the hall.

Inside the small conference room, the overhead lights hummed momentarily before casting a bright glare over a wood veneer table. A small corner shelf held an assortment of paper cups, highlighters, pens, napkins, and extension cords. A white projection screen hung on the front wall, and an oversized chalkboard decorated the right wall. He unrolled the paper onto the table. Melody held a hand over her mouth and covered a yawn.

"Late night?" He placed his cell phone and the cup of pens on opposite sides of the blueprint.

"Yep." She blinked. "I stayed up watching the MN Twinkles baseball game."

"Wasn't that a great game?" Clayton slipped a marker from his pocket.

This day might be salvageable. She nodded. "I still can't believe they tied the game up in the eighth inning. In the tenth inning, I was ready to shut the TV off when Burger hit the ball to deep center. Taylor made that flying leap…"

5

"Sorry." Paula stepped through the doorway with two cups of coffee. "I should have warned you, don't get the Boss Lady talking about baseball, unless you plan to be here all day. If you need anything else, you'll find me at my desk."

"Thanks for the coffee." Clayton held up his mug. "And the heads-up."

Holding the warm paper cup with both hands, Mel took a big gulp. *Lukewarm and bitter.* She watched Clayton mark the blueprint. *Mid-to-late thirties, sure of his work, mischievous grin, likes baseball, but he bites his nails.*

He drummed his fingers against the side of his mug. "Is your husband a baseball fan, too?"

"I'm a widow." She glanced at her gold wedding band. "And Harold was never a sports fan."

He set his cup down and made eye contact. "My condolences."

Swallowing the lump in her throat, she blinked. *If he knew me better, would he rest a hand on my forearm or pat my shoulder?* She took a sip of coffee. "Thank you. Harold passed away three years ago in December. Only fifty-two, he suffered a massive heart attack while shoveling snow."

His gaze softened. "So young."

"You always think you'll have a lifetime to make plans, and in a flash, everything changes."

As he brushed a dark curl from his forehead, the corners of his mouth curved into an infectious smirk. "I know. Yesterday, everyone said, you have your whole life ahead of you." He shook his head. "Now, all I hear is…you're not getting any younger."

An unexpected chuckle slipped between her lips.

"Unless you just turned forty-one, then everyone tells you the forties are the new twenties. So, I am getting younger."

"Forty, no way."

Is he flirting? Do guys still know how to do that? Or is everything prearranged on dating apps? Does his profile mention a magnificent smile and a cute dimple? Evening walks beneath star-studded skies?

"You, okay?"

Inhaling deeply, she backed away from the table. *Paula! All her talk about chance and romance.* She twisted the corners of her mouth into a smile. "It's been an endless week."

Stepping closer, he arched his right eyebrow and winked. "I might have what you need." He patted his back pocket.

Is he coming on to me like a character from an outdated sitcom? Mel shifted onto her heels.

His smile turned crooked. "Normally, I'd make the offer to Bill." He slipped a hand into his back pocket and took out a couple of tickets. "But since he's not here... Would you like to see the Twinkles game tonight? I've got four tickets and only need two."

"I'd love to, but my sister is deployed, and I'm currently the caretaker for my six-year-old niece."

"No problem. I'm bringing my godchild, Jack. He's a typical ten-year-old. He'll sit with his arms tightly folded across his chest, or he'll narrate play-by-play actions with a mouthful of popcorn."

"I know." Her voice raised an octave—*finally, someone who can relate to caring for someone else's child.* "Some days, I only have to say two words, and Kansas goes from smiling to sulking. I can't imagine what she'll be like as a teenager."

He placed the tickets into Melody's hand.

She held them up and read the seat and section. "Wow." She waved the tickets. "These seats are along the third baseline, row seven. We'll be right above the dugout."

"Yep."

"I haven't been to a game in years. Thank you." She raised her right hand.

He stepped back to the table.

What, no fist pump or high five?

Tapping the blueprint, he beckoned with a shift in his gaze.

She slipped the tickets into her back pocket.

"Now, what about the electrical outlets? Do you have a preference for the locations?"

Standing beside him, she inhaled, a subtle scent of red cedar with a slight citrus tinge teasing her senses. *Nice.* She leaned over, peering at the drawing. "I know we'll need enough for eight cubicles, my office, plus a plug-in for the printer station and copier."

He penciled in some notes. "Overhead lighting?"

"Yes, definitely lights."

"Of course." He snickered. "But any preference as to type or placement?"

"Florescent lights?" She shrugged.

"When you said you had limited construction knowledge, I thought you were joking."

"I am a quality assurance manager." She tossed back her shoulders. "Overseeing a team that detects and solves coding problems with software updates." After circling her face with a finger, she glared. "Do I look like Melody, the builder?"

The tip of his middle finger brushed his lips and muffled his words.

"What?" Mel tensed and leaned closer.

"Sorry." He turned his palms up and shrugged. "I didn't mean to sound, so… I appreciate your help." He stuffed his right hand into his pocket. "Melody, I realize they tossed you into this situation. I don't want to make more work for you."

Is he serious or patronizing me? She gazed into his steady brown eyes. *He looks sincere.*

Pulling his hand from his pocket, he threaded his fingers through his curls. "I'm not the most articulate, but I am good at my job. I know what I'm doing. Do you trust me?"

Slowly exhaling, she released the tension from her shoulders. "Sorry. I had a tough morning. I'll trust you, because you like baseball. But if we end up working in the dark, it's on you."

"You'll have great lights and enough outlets. I'll tackle the remodeling details and keep you updated on the progress. How does that sound?"

"Sounds like a deal." Strong, calloused fingers lightly embraced her right hand as she held Clayton's gaze. A flutter in her stomach created an unaccustomed sensation. Dropping his hand, she shuffled back a step. *Butterflies at my age.*

"It should be a good game."

A knock sounded, and Paula stepped through the door. She darted her gaze around the room, drawing her eyebrows together. "Do you need me to order lunch?"

"No, we're just wrapping up." Mel motioned toward the door. "But thanks for checking." She turned her attention back to Clay as he gathered his blueprint.

9

It will be a great game.

"See you at seven, Mel." He brushed past.

"Yep, can't wait." Grinning, she stepped out of the office with Paula and watched him disappear down the hallway.

"Soooo."

Mel slapped a hand to her chest. "You scared me half to death. I forgot you were still here."

"Apparently." Paula tapped her toe. "What's the 'see you at seven' all about? Please don't tell me you're working late, again."

"He had extra tickets to the baseball game."

"I can't believe it." Paula swung her hips and raised her arms like a solar hula doll on a dashboard. "A tall, handsome man waltzes into the office and invites you to a baseball game. He has to be Mr. Right. Do you need someone to babysit Kansas?"

"No, Kansas is coming, and Clayton is bringing his ten-year-old godchild."

"Your first double date." Paula clapped.

"It's not a date. I am going to a Twinkles game with a guy who has extra tickets."

"Who is tall, handsome, and has a sexy smile."

"Not appropriate." Melody glanced around to make sure the conversation wasn't overheard.

"My bad." Paula laughed.

Mel fanned her warm cheeks. *Suddenly, I wish I could be inappropriate.*

Chapter Two

"Boss Lady. Five o'clock on a Friday. Let's get moving." Paula hovered in the doorway.

"What?" Mel rolled her chair back from the monitors on Bill's desk. "Five o'clock already?"

"Yes, hurry, or you won't have time to get ready. Do you have anything to wear?"

Mel shut down the computer and grabbed her laptop. "Yep."

"Really?" Paula cocked her head. "What?"

"Clothes." She chuckled.

Paula rolled her eyes. "If anything comes up and you need me, text."

"Okay." Mel followed her down the dark, dusty hallway.

Paula leaned forward, tapped the up arrow, and the elevator door opened.

"This morning, the doors wouldn't even budge." Mel shook her head. "So, do you and your magic touch have any plans for this weekend?"

"You know me, just volunteering at the dog shelter and going to the gym."

"Have you ever tried a dating app?"

"Pleasssse." Paula curled her lip as they exited the elevator. "I am a hopeless romantic. Who wants to stalk strangers on their phones when you can pursue them in their natural habitat?"

"I guess." Mel smirked as she held the lobby door open. "I hear you can learn a lot about a man by the way he bags poop."

"Funny." Paula swung her hips as they crossed the cobblestone street. "Besides, there's a lot of action in squatting and scooping, and I can see if he gets back up."

"Do you always get front-row parking?" Mel asked as they stopped by Paula's bright-red sports utility vehicle with a dashboard full of yellow ducks.

She nodded. "I'm pretty sure this used to be your spot."

Before Kansas, she would arrive first to work and claim the premier parking spot. Mel tilted her head. Something had changed. Being the first person at work no longer seemed like an honor, but she wanted to tease Paula. "Well, don't get too comfortable. In a couple of months, I'll be reclaiming my space."

"Who knows? Maybe you'll find someone else to give you a hard time in the mornings." Paula shouted. "Now, that's funny."

Instead of responding, Mel rolled her eyes and wandered to the back of the lot, humming a Bruno Mars song. Before driving away, she tuned her station to love songs. "My love," she belted as she drove to pick up her niece.

At the entrance of the day care, she waited for half a dozen cars to exit before pulling into the parents' lot. An oversized banner announcing openings for their summer day camp now hung above the entrance. She pulled open the glass doors of the converted fitness center and scents of week-old gym clothes, sour milk, and waxy crayons assaulted her. She wrinkled her nose.

Fridays smell the worst. She rushed to the recreation room and spotted Kansas sitting with her backpack.

"Auntie, Auntie." She raced forward, dragging a pink backpack and a jacket as her dark, shoulder-length curls bounced.

Mel braced herself for impact as Kansas slammed into her thighs. "Good to see you, too. Ready to go?" She hugged the bundle of energy.

"Yes." Kansas broke free.

"Wait, slow down. Remember the rules. No running." Mel shrugged apologetically at the young woman with blue highlights in her blonde hair. "I guess everyone's glad today's Friday, and I won't forget to sign her out."

The young woman grinned and waved.

Mel stepped outside and gulped in the fresh air. She grasped Kansas' hand. "You have to hold my hand in the parking lot."

"Oh, Auntie, you worry too much. I'm big."

She shook her head and kept a tight grip on her niece until they stood beside the car.

Kansas scampered into the backseat and buckled her booster seat. "See."

"Yep, you are all grown up, but I promised your mom I'd always hold your hand in the parking lot." Mel slid inside and started the car.

"Alyssa and me got invited to Erica's pool party."

Mel exited the lot and merged into traffic. "That's nice. When?"

"Tonight. I already told Alyssa and Erica I could go."

In the past nine months, Kansas went from a shy, clingy kid to an independent young girl. She glanced in the rearview mirror. "Aren't you a little social butterfly?" Mel drew her eyebrows together. *Opal is missing out on another first with her daughter.* She swallowed. A half mile from the house, Mel's words boomed against the windshield. "Wait, I almost forgot. I'm taking you to a baseball game tonight."

"No! I'm going to the outdoor pool party."

Mel glanced into the rearview mirror.

She shook her head and sat with crossed arms over her chest. "No, baseball. Erica's."

"I already have the tickets."

Kansas kicked the back of Mel's seat. "I'm not going, and you can't make me."

Mel took a deep breath and softened her voice. "You come to the baseball game tonight, and we'll do whatever you want tomorrow night." After a minute of silence, she glanced in the rearview mirror.

Kansas vigorously shook her head.

She drummed her fingers on the steering wheel. *What would Opal do?* She sucked on her bottom lip. *I'm not Opal, and I'm not a mom.* She sighed. *Life will be easier when Opal returns and my only job is spoiling Kansas.* Mel smiled. *I'll take a managerial approach— firm and direct.* "You are going to the baseball game. If I had known about Erica's party, I wouldn't have accepted the tickets. But I didn't know. So, we're going."

After waiting and hearing no response, she glanced in the mirror. Kansas' expression mimicked her mother's hatching-a-plan face. *Right eyebrow cocked high and lips pursed tight.*

"So," Kansas said. "A person shouldn't break promises, and I promised Alyssa."

Focused on the road, she held her breath.

"Maybe," Kansas cooed. "I could stay at Alyssa's house." She clapped. "I could go to the pool party, and you could go to your stupid ball game."

Dang, a sleepover. Why didn't I think of that? Mel exhaled and glanced back, catching the moment the grin on her niece's face turned into a toothy smile. *She tricked me. Am I that easy to manipulate? Or is Kansas destined for an upper management position?*

****

Mel drove into the driveway of her suburban home. Like most of her neighbors, she had an attached two-door garage but parked outside. Unlike her neighbors, her garage didn't have a boat or a snowmobile. Instead, she had boxes from her late husband and Opal's thirty large, black plastic bins.

She sighed and kicked at the overgrown weeds lining her driveway. *Tomorrow,* she vowed. *I'll send a check and my apologies to the lawn company.*

"Hurry, Auntie." Ignoring the door handle, Kansas added more handprints to the glass window on the front door.

"Wait." Melody rushed forward before Kansas added tiny shoe scuffs to the base of the black storm door.

The girl barged through the open door, dropped her backpack on the dated ceramic entry tiles, and fished Mel's phone from her purse. "What letter is she under?"

"A-l-y-s-s-a."

With pursed lips, she tapped in the letters. "It's ringing." She sang out, jumping and dancing like she scored the purple giraffe from the claw machine at the arcade.

Mel reached for the phone, and a few moments later, she nodded and disconnected. A long, slow sigh escaped from tight lips. *Alyssa's mom didn't ask about my game buddy or for a return favor on Saturday night.* "Pack up an overnight bag."

"I'm going to a party." Kansas skipped across the tiled entryway and down the hardwood floor hall, singing.

With the perfect outfit in mind, Mel slipped into her closet and pushed hangers aside until she spotted her Twinkles jersey. After sniffing nothing but the faded scent of dryer sheets, she pulled a denim skirt out from behind winter sweaters and leggings and danced to the dresser. She held the jersey above the skirt and glanced into the mirror. *This outfit looks better than my lucky pizza-stained Twinkles T-shirt and shorts.* Mel stepped into the hall. "Kansas, pack pj's, a swimsuit, and a towel. I'll be in the shower."

"Okay, Auntie."

Twenty minutes later, Mel found Kansas dragging her backpack and sleeping bag down the hall. *At least, the floors are getting dusted.*

Kansas slammed into Mel with a hug. "Auntie, you're the best."

After nine months of caring for Kansas, she now understood the heartbreak of not hugging your child daily. She returned the hug, ruffling her soft, dark curls. *Opal is missing so much.*

She heard her phone chirp and checked the message. "Alyssa's mom will be here in five minutes. Are you ready?"

Kansas nodded.

When they stepped out the front door, Mel checked

her reflection in the door. She ran her fingers through her hair. *I look pretty good.* Hand in hand, she raced with Kansas to Alyssa's van. "Be good." She stooped to hug Kansas.

She returned a hasty hug. "I will."

With tightly drawn lips, she watched Kansas crawl next to Alyssa in the van and leave without a backward glance or even a wave. *Watching your child leave with someone else stinks. Opal must be going through hell.*

She hustled back inside and grabbed her phone, purse, and car keys. Once inside her car, she cranked up the tunes on her radio, and within an hour, she was driving into downtown Minneapolis. The builders constructed the Twinkles stadium in the middle of the warehouse district, the Mississippi River, and the downtown skyline. The tall buildings made a beautiful backdrop. People strolled down the sidewalks in the early summer evening, chatting and laughing. Mel waited for a group of pedestrians to clear the driveway before pulling into the parking ramp. She drove up to the second level. *Nothing is inappropriate about accepting tickets. Besides, I'm at least five years older than him.* On the fourth level, she found an open spot and parked.

She drew in a breath and swiped her palms across her denim skirt—*nothing more than a guy with extra tickets to the game.* She ran the applicator of *Just Kissed* over her lips, exhaled, and smiled at her reflection in the rearview mirror.

Fifteen minutes later, she passed through security. She turned her head in every direction.

"Programs for sale," vendors called out.

"Get your ice-cold beer right here," others shouted.

In the corridor, the smell of popcorn turned to hot dogs, then to the sweet scent of freshly made waffle cones and spun cotton candy. *Next time, I'm bringing Kansas.* The thought of her smiling face, wanting to try the foods and purchase souvenirs, made Mel sigh—*next time.*

She slipped back into the crowd of red, navy, gold, and white attire, following the signs to section one hundred and eighteen. At the top of the landing, she looked past the rows of blue plastic seats to the field. Squinting, she spotted the players standing by their dugouts. Eager to watch the game, she quickened her step and passed several more rows before she spotted Clayton standing with a woman with blonde hair and red, pouty lips.

Once again, I'm the third wheel, but this time, I look like a cheerleader. She clenched her hands. *I want to see the game. He invited me.* She sucked on her bottom lip.

"Hey, Lady, any day now," groaned the person standing behind her.

Before she took a step, she heard her name.

"Melody!" Clay waved his arms. "Melody, down here."

After forcing the corners of her mouth to form a smile, she cautiously descended the remaining stairs.

Clay brushed the tip of his thumb along his bottom lip. "Melody, I'd like you to meet Brenda."

She extended her right hand to the woman standing next to him. Someone who shook hands like a European kissed hello—all air and no contact.

Brenda brushed against Clayton's body and gazed into his eyes. "I thought you told me she was bringing a kid."

After several weight shifts, Mel smiled. "A last-minute invite to a pool party. I hope you don't mind." When no one objected, she plopped into the empty seat next to Clayton.

He remained standing with his hands dangling, and Brenda draped around him.

Mel watched the muscles in his jaw work overtime. *He doesn't look happy; if he's not careful, he'll chew a hole through his cheek.* She stood. "Do you guys want anything before the game starts? Soda, beer?"

"I'd like a beer," Brenda said.

He removed Brenda's arm and stepped closer to Mel. "My treat. A pale ale, pilsner, or a craft beer?" He rested a hand on Mel's jersey sleeve and nodded toward the stairs.

The warmth of his touch sent shivers of delight to the pit of her stomach. "I'm not picky, but if they have a light beer, that would be fine."

He tilted his head toward the aisle. "Would you like to come with me?"

"I'll go." Brenda repositioned her body against Clayton. "She looks tired and probably wants to sit and rest."

"Yeah, I'll wait here." Mel leaned back against the chair, pulling her legs in to let them pass. She glanced at Clay as his leg brushed her knees. He made a silly face, tilted his head towards Brenda, and winked.

She slumped farther into her seat as the two ascended the stairs. *Is he flirting? Is the woman not his girlfriend?* She shifted and tugged at the hem of her skirt as she texted.

—Paula, one touch from Mr. Tall, Dark, and

Handsome awoke feelings I've never experienced.—

A moment later, Paula replied with a slew of love emojis.

Chuckling, Mel composed her response.

—Oh, never mind. It turns out I'm only gassy. LOL—

Twenty minutes later, Brenda's patronizing laughs jerked Mel back to reality.

"Slide down." Brenda motioned with a hand.

"Let me sit next to her." Clayton stretched an arm out.

She blocked his advancement. "She'd rather talk to me. Her niece is living with her, and I'm a single parent. We have a lot in common."

Mel leaned around Brenda and narrowed her gaze at Clayton. *How dare he tell her my life story?*

Brenda took a beer from Clayton and handed one to Mel. "He only told me about your niece because he wanted to know if Jack was ready. Of course, I had spaced out about the game and let Jack go to a friend's house."

"Oh." Mel took a large swallow of the beer. She couldn't decide if she'd rather watch Brenda paw him or listen to her non-stop talking.

After the second inning, Brenda turned back to Clayton.

Mel exhaled, leaned forward, and focused on the field.

At the bottom of the fifth inning, Brenda stood. "Excuse us, Clayton. We're headed to the little girls' room."

"You go. The line will be long, and I don't want to miss any of the game." Mel cringed as Brenda stormed past.

Clay moved over, brushing a hand against her forearm as he sat. "I'm so sorry. The only reason we're still friends is because of my godson, Jack."

The crowd suddenly roared and cheered.

Mel turned from Clay to the big screen, but instead of seeing a replay of a fantastic play, she stared at the oversized image of herself and Clay.

"Kiss, kiss," people chanted.

Mel swallowed and nudged Clay. "We're on the kiss camera." His lips brushed against her mouth. She lowered her eyelids. *I'm kissing him.* His warm lips lingered, the kiss deepened, and she could feel her heart racing. The crowd noise faded. His arms wrapped around her, and instead of resisting, she melted into his embrace. She struggled to get closer, but the armrest blocked her advances. The pressure from his lips lessened, and she peeked through her eyelashes into his intense gaze. Afraid he'd see her desire, she closed her eyes.

"Excuse me!" Brenda said.

Mel glanced over at her towering figure and frozen facial expression and braced herself for a confrontation. She tried to put a little space between herself and Clay, but his arm remained firmly around her shoulders.

"Did you see us on the kiss camera?" Clayton asked.

"You put on quite the show." Brenda stood above them with both hands on her hips.

"Down in front!" a man yelled.

"Kiss, kiss," the older gal with too many plastic beer cups by her feet chanted.

Brenda's lip curled like a hooked fish. "I want to

go home. Now." She stomped.

Clay stood and followed behind her swaying hips as she stormed the steps. He stopped, turned, and held up an index finger.

Mel arched an eyebrow and flashed a smile. *Is he coming back?*

Chapter Three

The noise from the cheering fans faded as Mel shifted in the stadium seat. *Clayton kissed me. And I kissed Clay back.* She brushed a finger over her bottom lip, and the tingle of his touch remained. She leaned back, wrapping her arms around her waist, and sighed.

"That was some kiss," the woman with the empty beer cups said. "And then you let him slip through your fingers. *Tsk, tsk.*"

At the unwanted attention, Mel squirmed. She didn't want to encourage a conversation and hoped a slight smile would suffice. At the sound of a bat cracking, Mel jumped to her feet along with the rest of the fans.

The ball sailed toward the left-field stands before veering into foul territory, and the crowd let out a collective sigh. A flash of warmth penetrated her forearm. She jerked her head. "Clay." She peered around him. *He's alone.* She smiled. *And he's looking at me in the same way I watched the foul ball.* She licked her bottom lip.

"Hopefully, I'll talk you into giving me a ride back? She took my truck home." He tilted his head and winked.

Lost in his gaze, Mel swayed and reached back for the armrest. "Of course, I'll give you a ride." She sat, envisioning the two of them in the front seat of her sedan, locked in an embrace, while struggling to do more within the confines of her car.

"Good." He sat next to her.

Images of the big bad wolf from *Little Red Riding Hood* flashed through her thoughts. *I feel like the wolf in Grandma's clothes, wanting to eat up the unsuspecting visitor. Clay should run after Brenda.* After several more sideways glances, Mel squirmed. She crossed her legs and jiggled a foot, but nothing helped to dispel the anticipation of the drive home and the possibility of a goodnight kiss. She struggled to stay seated until the end of the game.

The MN Twinkles won four to three, which added to her excitement. As they waded with the crowd through the exit, Clay held her hand.

"So, where to?" He glanced up at the rooftop patio bar across the street. "Are you in a rush to get home?"

The warm summer breeze and the kiss had her wanting to stay out all night. She gazed at the twinkling overhead lights. "No, there is nothing or no one to hurry home to."

He let go of her hand and draped an arm around her shoulders.

She stopped dead in her tracks. "Is this allowed?"

"What?" His single word caressed her skin as his fingers brushed the hair from her neck.

"Kissing? Drinking?"

"You told me you're older than twenty-one." He winked.

"Much older, but that's not what I mean. Bill hired you, and I'm taking his place. Could this be an ethics violation?" The moment Mel uttered the words, she wished she could swallow them back down. She wasn't a rule-breaker. But she didn't want to say goodnight, either.

His right arm slipped off her shoulder. "If you were Bill, I wouldn't have kissed you, but I would have invited you for a drink."

"Thankfully, I'm not Bill." Mel closed her eyes. *I can't believe I said that.* She peeked through her eyelashes. *He's still here after my stupid comment.* "Okay, one drink, and then I'm taking you home."

His left eyebrow jetted up.

"Not my home." She pressed her hands against her warm cheeks. "No. I'll drop you off at your house."

"You have the best smile when you're flustered."

"I've been experiencing a lot of flusters lately." She fanned her face.

Buzz-buzz-buzz.

She recognized the sound and tilted her head. "Probably Paula is checking up on me." She took the phone from her purse and frowned. "Ed Furlow?" She could feel her pulse quicken. "Alyssa's parents. They're watching Kansas." She swiped twice before the phone connected. "Hello, hello."

"Melody, it's Mary. The girls had a great time, but now they have upset stomachs but no fevers. Probably nothing more than too much pizza and pool water."

"The game just ended. Tell Kansas I'll be there in an hour." She disconnected.

"Trouble?" Clayton asked.

"I need to pick up Kansas. It's either something she ate or the excitement of her first overnight."

"You don't have to drive me to Rockerville. I'll call WeRide."

"I live off of Fourth on Stonehenge in the same

subdivision." Mel drew her eyebrows lower as she studied him. *What is a young single guy doing living in a suburb? He should live in a downtown condo, partying, and doing whatever people do nowadays.*

"No way! We're in the same neighborhood." He raised an eyebrow. "I live at Eighth and Flagstone."

"By the park?" Mel studied his response.

"Yeah, a few blocks away." He nodded.

"I've taken my niece to that park. Don't call WeRide. I'll drive by your place on my way to pick up Kansas."

Fifty minutes later, she stopped in front of his house.

He leaned in close.

Anticipating a kiss, she wet her lips.

He grasped her hand. "I hope we can do this again. I had a great time."

"Me too, Clay." She nodded as cool air replaced his warm touch.

With a click of his key ring, he illuminated a brick-and-stucco two-story house with a front porch. "Thanks for the ride, Mel." He paused, making eye contact before stepping out and shutting the door.

Mel slumped against the seat. "He had a great time," she repeated his words, savoring them like sweet ice cream. "A great time with me." The words drifted from her lips like a song. *I am giddy.* She shifted into gear. *I've never been a giddy person.*

As she walked up to Alyssa's house, Mel forced a smile from her face, suddenly feeling guilty for having the best night of her life while Kansas was sick. Before she could ring the doorbell, the door opened.

"Auntie, you're here." Kansas rushed forward with

her backpack. "They had a slide into the pool, and we ate pizza."

After thanking Mary, she and Kansas walked down the driveway.

"My tummy's better."

Mel buckled Kansas' booster seat. "Probably too much pizza." *Or homesickness.* "I'm glad you're okay. Let's go home."

At home, she tucked Kansas into bed and read half a bedtime story before noticing her niece was asleep. She tucked the book back onto the shelf, and images of her and Clay on the big screen sent renewed warmth through her.

I'll bust if I don't tell someone, but if I tell Paula, things might get awkward at the office. She brushed a thumb across her lips. *The lips Clay kissed.*

She rushed to the spare bedroom she used for an office and poured her heart onto four blank sheets. The excitement of the evening had her right hand rushing across the page. She hoped Opal could decipher her messy handwriting. Before sealing the envelope, she added some artwork and a PS about how Kansas would always be the number one priority. She wrote on the inside flap.

Be Safe, Be Careful, Be Proud, and tell everyone in your unit, thank you for your service and sacrifice from Kansas and me.

Despite a night spent rolling in and out of reality, Mel awoke with newfound energy. She didn't even wait for a cup of coffee before rushing to the mailbox with Opal's letter. She set the sealed, stamped envelope into the black metal mailbox and lifted the red flag.

For the first time, she didn't spend the weekend

thinking of work schedules and project deadlines. Instead, her thoughts revolved around Clay. The remembrance of his kiss sent tingles down her spine. *He kissed me in front of the crowd, and I liked it.* She brushed a finger against her lips. Mel tossed clothes into the dryer and imagined herself nuzzled in Clay's embrace. She found the nineties radio station on her stereo and vacuumed, mopped, and dusted the hours away. Before the last song in the top forty hits played, she'd finished every room in the house.

Saturday night, Kansas stayed up hours past her bedtime, watching an animated cartoon and eating popcorn. When she nodded off for the third time, Mel carried her to bed and kissed her dimpled cheek goodnight.

She tossed in another load of laundry and replayed the memories from Friday night. *Should I have let him kiss me on the sidewalk after the game? Would one more kiss have made a difference?* Mel questioned every action and reaction from Friday as she mindlessly refolded the underwear in her drawer. *Do I even want a man in my life?*

For the rest of the weekend, Mel played with different scenarios. If Clay continued to show interest, should she pursue him or pretend she had no interest in kissing him again? Did she want to spend her nights alone? Her previous marriage was more of a partnership, not a heated love affair. She and Harold enjoyed conversations, dinner, and an occasional movie, but besides these simple securities, they shared little else.

If she were honest with herself, their marriage lacked sexual intimacy, but she never worried about mood swings, excessive drinking, unemployment, or infidelity. Harold was predictable and kind, and she cherished their time together. After he died, she was lonely and missed the comfort he provided.

After Clay's kiss, she didn't experience emptiness but rather a hunger emerging from the recesses of her heart. But for what? She wasn't sure. For the first time, she balked at settling for whatever life dealt; she wanted more…so much more.

On Monday, she twisted off her gold wedding band and nestled the ring in her top dresser drawer with the other items she cherished. She took a deep breath, exhaled, and smiled. *Time to stop hiding in the past.* She took her time getting ready for work and paused at her reflection. *I'm smiling. I'm eager to go to the office.* She shook her head. *Not my typical reaction.* She broke the seal on the bottle of her favorite perfume Opal had sent last Christmas and sniffed. Notes of sweet, sun-ripened pears, shifting to a subtle scent of vanilla, filled the air. Twenty minutes later, she danced into Kansas' room, singing, "Wake up, sleepyhead."

Beneath soft curls, eyelids fluttered. She sat and rubbed her eyes. "You're beautiful, and you smell good."

"I always look like this."

She shook her head. "Today, you look nice."

"Thank you." She brushed the tousled, dark brown curls from her forehead. "You're beautiful, too." Mel placed a light kiss on her left dimple. *Will I see Clay today? Will he lean in close and think I smell nice, too?* A surge of excitement propelled her out the door. "Let's go."

Chapter Four

On Monday, they arrived at child care with time to spare.

"Auntie, I want to show you the new games in the recreation room and the picture I'm painting."

For fifteen minutes, Mel nodded and smiled as she followed her around, but after saying good-bye and slipping into her car, she no longer had Kansas on her mind. The construction crew would be on the fourth floor, and Bill's office was in the basement, but if Clay was interested, he'd find an excuse.

And if he wanders downstairs, do I flirt, encourage romance, or remain professional? Of course, the logical and responsible choice would disappoint Paula. Mel laughed. She probably had them head over heels in love and planning a romantic wedding.

Today, she had no trouble finding a place to park, and the elevator rushed to open when she pressed the button. In the basement, she glanced around before stepping into the corridor. Mel tippy-toed fast past Paula's empty desk and slipped into her office unnoticed. She exhaled and refrained from doing a happy dance. *I snuck past Paula and her romance radar. One glance and she'll know I kissed Clay.*

When she gazed at her workspace, the thrill of slipping something past Paula faded. Today would allow no time for daydreaming. She sank into her chair, flipped the switch on the computer, and cringed. With one hundred and seventeen unread messages, tension clenched her jaw as she resisted the urge to abandon her chair and search for more coffee. At the sound of shoes coming down the hallway, Mel glanced away from the screen, exhaling as she braced herself for the questions.

"Boss Lady." Paula stuck her head through the doorway. "You must have snuck by this morning. I was waiting for you."

After stretching her arms above her head, Mel stood and eased the tension from her neck.

The paisley print, pink and green minidress Paula wore swished as she walked closer to the desk. "Hmm." She grinned. "Well, there's still a little glow left from this weekend."

"The game was great. Good seats. MN Twinkles won."

"Any home runs?" Paula raised an eyebrow twice.

At the memory of the kiss, heat rushed from the pit of Mel's stomach to her cheeks.

"Yes." Paula pumped her fist.

"Have you started clogging lessons?" Mel fanned her flaming face.

"Now that's funny." She performed a twirl and side-shuffled out the door.

"Good morning." A deep voice chuckled.

"Sorry," Paula squeaked. "I didn't see you."

Recognizing Clay's voice, Mel tried to swallow. *Do I shake his hand, hug him, or wink?* After mentally undressing him for the better part of the weekend, she no longer knew what was appropriate.

"Got a minute?" Clay smiled and stepped through the doorway, wearing a denim shirt tucked into the waistband of his fitted jeans. "Morning, Mel." A dimple on his left cheek appeared as the tip of his tongue wet his lips.

Is he thinking about the passionate kiss we shared? He's like a magnet, and I'm the refrigerator. I want him stuck on me. She tugged at the hem of her blouse. *I'll need a stronger antiperspirant.*

His brows knitted together, and his gaze shifted to the floor. He slipped his hands into his pockets and glanced up. "How's your niece?"

"She's good. Nothing more than too much pizza; maybe being a little homesick. Kids get so excited at their first overnights." Mel clamped her lips tightly. *I'm rambling like an idiot.*

Clay shifted and stepped closer. His thigh brushed the edge of the desk.

Certain he could hear her heart pounding, she redirected her attention to a spot on the wall.

"I was wondering if I could take you to lunch at noon." He gestured with his hands. "Afterward, I'd like to show you some lighting options."

"I'll have to check." Mel directed her comments toward the hallway. "Some of Bill's appointments didn't merge onto my calendar. I know you can hear me, Paula."

"You're free for lunch," she hollered.

Maybe this isn't such a good idea. Thinking about him was one thing, but lunching, gazing into his eyes while discussing lighting options—she nodded. "Uh-uh, yes." Movement outside her door caught her attention. She turned and squinted.

Paula strutted back and forth past the office opening, pumping her arms and twirling her hands.

Don't let him turn around and see Paula's antics. She closed her eyes.

"Is everything okay?"

Mel opened her eyes and saw him cock his head toward the hallway. She grinned and mouthed, *Paula.*

He spun around and stepped through the doorway.

Eyes wide, Paula skidded to a stop. "Oh." Pink tinged her cheeks. "Gotta go."

"Now that's funny." Mel giggled as she waved to them both. They had kept the exchange of pleasantries professional. Yet she could feel her heart beat hard against her chest—the way he said—*noon.*

She reminded herself to exhale. *Nothing more than middle-aged hormones.* She deleted over a dozen emails. As she composed a response, she heard a throat clearing and glanced up to see Paula standing before her desk.

"I cleared your afternoon appointments." Paula moved her eyebrows like a hula girl.

She'd let Paula indulge in her romantic fantasies. "If that's all, I've got a lot of work."

"I just wanted you to know." Paula shrugged.

With effort, Mel refocused, returning calls and cleaning up emails. She sent a quick poll to her employees, asking for preferences for overhead lights, which was a mistake because everyone had a different opinion. As she searched online for lighting options, she heard shoes tapping.

"It's almost noon. What are you doing here?" Paula shook her head. "Get. Go."

Where did the time go? She had forgotten about Clay and their lunch date. She pushed back from the desk and jumped from her chair like a superhero. *Once again, my hormones are back under my control.* But when she stepped into the lobby, the sight of the dark-haired, brown-eyed man caused an ache. She wanted to touch him and feel his lips kiss her.

Today, she didn't feel old. She stepped outdoors and squinted. "I forget about the sun working in the windowless basement. I need to get out more." With a tilt of her head, she bathed in the warmth.

"Nothing like sunshine." He smiled and directed her to a white pickup truck with a *Construction Dunn Wright* decal across the side. "I wish I had a convertible or at least a sunroof. Hopefully, you don't mind the work truck."

"No, not at all." She climbed in, turned, and caught him watching her. Instead of blushing, she flashed a toothy grin. *I'm enjoying his interest.*

A moment later, she studied him as he climbed into the front seat. He entered with strength and grace. His body was lean but not skinny. His T-shirt accentuated his muscular arms and broad shoulders, and the truck smelled of cedar and citrus. She smiled as the fingers on his left hand tapped the steering wheel while his right hand turned the ignition. Was he worried? She never imagined she could make a man like Clay nervous. Another explanation must exist.

"You ready?" he asked.

She buckled her seat belt. *Is he in some sort of trouble? Maybe he is a gambler and needs money.* She frowned. *Will he trick me into purchasing the most expensive lights or pad the bills with extra work hours?* She made a mental note to read the contract Bill had signed and to be careful with what she approved.

"Relax." He adjusted the visor as the sun bounced

through the windshield and highlighted the gold flecks in his eyes. "I'm taking you to lunch, not to the dentist."

She tensed and drew her eyebrows together. "I'm not the person invited to lunch. I'm the employee huddled in her office for ten to twelve hours. If Paula didn't order lunch, half of my co-workers would never eat." She forced her hands to stay folded in her lap instead of crossing them tightly across her chest.

Not hearing Clay respond with a witty rebuttal or a distracting anecdote, she rethought her response. Had she overreacted? Was this how Clay typically acted? She wanted to break the awkward silence but couldn't think of one thing to say and shifted her gaze to look out the window.

Fifteen minutes later, he drove into a parking lot crowded with pickup trucks. A small white diner stood alone at the corner of the industrial park. A faded blue sign hung off the side of the building.

But Mel couldn't read the name. His sudden quietness had her regretting saying *yes* to this lunch invitation. She wanted to ask him for a ride back to the office but couldn't find the right words.

He opened his door and stepped outside.

After fumbling with her seat belt, she hustled around the truck and barely avoided colliding into Clay.

"I hope you don't mind having lunch at this diner. The good food and service make up for the lack of fancy ambiance." He shuffled his feet and stuffed his hands into his pockets.

"Yeah, looks good." She ground her back molars together. *Why am I always so agreeable?*

At the entrance, a man with sleeve tattoos held open the door. As he made eye contact, he grinned.

"Enjoy." He winked.

A flutter stirred her heart. *Did he just flirt?* Mel glanced back. Even though she wasn't interested, the brief exchange warmed her.

Inside, the restaurant had a retro yet authentic vibe, reminding her of a cafeteria. The sounds of silverware jiggling, dishes banging, and boisterous male voices echoing in conversation.

"Follow me." A server motioned as she weaved around a dozen occupied tables and booths. "One minute." She bent over the table with a spray bottle and dish rag.

Sandwiched between the server's backside and Clay's muscular thighs, Mel stood motionless. A warm hand brushed her shoulder. She turned.

"You have me feeling like a tongue-tied teenager. I hope the drive wasn't too awkward."

"Sit." The server motioned them toward the red tufted chairs. "I'll be right back to get your order."

Mel sat and picked up the laminated menu.

"Are we good?" Clay shifted in his chair. Concern etched across his facial features.

"Yeah, you also make me nervous." The smile she flashed was a poor substitute for the hug she'd like to give him.

The server returned.

Mel ordered a cheeseburger, fries, and a soda.

He ordered a mixed salad with grilled chicken and dressing on the side.

After the waitstaff left, Mel crumpled the edge of her paper napkin. "I feel like I'm the one who should have ordered a salad."

"My grandmother, Edith, spent a lifetime pleasing

36

everyone and never had time to enjoy life. She told me, you only get one life, live it."

"A wonderful sentiment. My dad was the opposite of your grandma. He'd grumble, 'why should I care about anyone when no one cares about me?' He was a bitter man. That might be why he had no friends."

"Yeah, I'm not sure where any of this is going. But enjoy your meal."

"Excuse me, folks. Hot plate." The server slid a sizzling burger in front of Mel.

The scent of grilled beef immediately stopped her inner chatter. "Mmm." She rolled her golden fry into a dish of ketchup. "Delicious."

"I guess the point of my story was moderation." He jabbed a lettuce leaf and tomato with his fork. "You know, a balance between worrying about what others think and not being considerate of others' feelings."

"Yeah." Mel nodded. She took another bite of her burger and smiled when he switched the conversation to baseball.

The server stopped by and inquired about desserts.

She shook her head and watched Clay also refuse anything more. After exiting the restaurant, she continued to chat about baseball. "The Royaltons? If you're still one of their fans, I'm no longer sure I can trust you." She paused next to the truck.

Clay held open the passenger door. "I was a Royaltons' fan. But after moving to the Twin Cities, I switched my loyalty to the MN Twinkles."

She climbed into the truck. "You lived in Missouri?"

He slid into the driver's seat. "Yep, until six years ago. Kansas City, Missouri, born and raised."

"Kansas. The same name as my niece."

He started the truck. "A great name. I bet she's a good kid."

"She is wonderful, but I'll be glad when her mom is back. I've always been the aunt, spoiling her on weekends, and now to assume the role of rule-maker and enforcer is tough."

He drove out of the parking lot. "I've always wanted kids."

"Never married?" Mel turned and studied him.

"Almost, but she left me at the altar," he mumbled.

The image of him standing in front of the church, waiting, tugged at her heart. "So…"

"Another time."

So, there'd be a next time. She grinned. *Did he have any other secrets?*

****

On the drive back from the Visual Comfort and Creative Lighting store, Mel pushed aside the thought of Clay standing in a church as she half-listened to him talking. *What do I do? What's Bill's budget? How much time can I spend on this remodel? Is the software testing still on schedule?*

After they parked, she thought about the lights. *Should I go with cheap lights and hope everyone can see their computers, or should I choose the new technology lights?* The truck door opened. She shook her head and climbed out of the cab. "I have a lot on my mind."

His thumb brushed her shoulder. "Don't worry about the lighting." He took a step back and shut the door.

She stood inches from him. The sun warmed her

skin, and he warmed her heart.

"After your input"—he gazed into her eyes—"I can make some decisions. And in the future, I'd suggest not asking your employees for ideas. Experience has taught me they never agree. Even if you could give them everything they wanted, you'd exceed your budget, and some still wouldn't be happy."

"Yeah." She nodded and wiped her damp palms against her thighs. They remained only inches apart. She took a deep breath. "Since we are practically neighbors..." Mel took another breath. "Would you like to come over on Saturday afternoon for chili dogs? I have the sports entertainment package. The MN Twinkles are playing the Royaltons."

Clay winked. "Sounds great, but you don't have to cook chili dogs. I'll bring dinner for three."

"Let me guess, Cobb salad." She shrugged. "Your loss. You've never had my chili dogs."

"Wait." He pulled a creased photo from his wallet.

She glanced at the obese teenager in a buzz cut. She drew her brows together, glancing from the photo to Clay.

"That was me in high school; I weighed over three hundred pounds." He nodded. "Yep, fat. I watch what I eat, but I don't judge what others eat. You make chili dogs, and I'll toss a salad together to complement the dogs."

Mel couldn't stop grinning as they walked through the parking lot and into the lobby.

He gave a half wave. "See you Saturday."

Watching Clay disappear into the stairwell, she covered her face with her hands. *When did I get so brave? My invitation to Clay will thrill Paula, but the thought makes me nervous.*

For the next three hours, Mel pushed thoughts of the impending date aside and focused on work until she heard footsteps. She glanced up as Paula popped into her office.

"Boss Lady, pull the plug. It's time to pick up Kansas."

"Thanks, Paula. I have no idea where my brain's been."

"You've got a lot to think about...job, Kansas, and now Mr. Tall Dark and Handsome. Hey, you never said how lunch went?"

As Mel shut things off, she told Paula about lunch.

"You invited him over to watch the game?" She shook her head as they stepped out of the elevator. "I didn't see that curve ball coming."

"Shhhh." Mel glanced around the lobby to ensure no other employees overheard the comment. She exhaled at the empty entryway, rushed outside, and squinted.

Paula jabbed her in the side with her elbow. "The sun's as bright as your smile. If this keeps up, I'll need sunglasses in the office."

"Ha, ha." She waved and headed across the parking lot. She heard Paula call her name and stopped.

"I can't even imagine Clay in your house." Paula did a fist pump.

Mel smiled as she walked to her car. She had no problem imagining Clay in her house. She moistened her lips. *Will he kiss me on Saturday?*

Chapter Five

In Gascon's lot, Mel slipped into her car with Paula's comment about Clay being in her house still echoing in her thoughts. The radio blared as the engine engaged. She turned the tunes down as she mentally filed away the tasks she needed to get done.

At the day care center, she spotted Kansas outside with two other girls. She resisted the urge to fist-pump like Paula. Today, Kansas wasn't the last kid picked up. Mel helped Kansas manage her backpack, lunchbox, and jacket.

"If you're happy…" Kansas sang and bounced all the way to the car.

Not wanting to break the mood, Mel hummed along. She put the car into gear and merged out into traffic. After a couple of blocks, she glanced into the rearview mirror. "What's up?"

"I asked Alyssa and McKenzie to sleep at our house on Saturday night. Their moms will call you later."

She tightened her grip on the steering wheel. "What? You can't invite people over. You need to ask permission first." The words sounded louder than Mel intended. But all she could think about was entertaining three kids. What if they got sick, injured, or started crying for their parents? Mel shook her head repeatedly.

"I asked their moms while I waited to get picked

up."

She glanced into the rearview mirror to make sure a thirteen-year-old hadn't swapped places with Kansas. Color returned to her knuckles as she relaxed her grip. "First, you ask me. If I say yes, then you can invite them over. But you can't have two friends sleep over, because I already invited someone to watch the baseball game on Saturday."

"Why can you have friends over and not me? You didn't ask permission."

"I'm the adult." Mel sighed. *Why do the tough questions come at the end of the day?*

"You always get to do what you want," Kansas yelled. "You're a mean adult. I hate you!"

Mel glanced over at a minivan full of children in the next lane.

The kids stared with their mouths wide open as they pointed fingers.

"I'm not mean. You went to the pool party last week. We played games last night. I took you shopping. You have a new backpack." Mel rolled her window down. "I bought her new shoes," she shouted toward the minivan before closing her window.

"Yeah, but you won't let me have friends." Kansas sobbed. "I want friends."

She drew in a few ragged breaths, and she switched to the right lane. The heated exchange reminded her of arguments with her sister. Kansas was as unreasonable as her mother. Sounds of sniffling and bubbling lips filled the air. Mel grimaced as her stomach balled into knots. "Hey, I know. Why don't we invite everyone to a movie with popcorn or maybe bowling?" She kept her voice cheerful and glanced into the rearview mirror.

"No, you're mean." Kansas sat with her arms folded across her chest. "I can't even lift a bowling ball. I hate you. I hate you."

After pulling into the driveway, Mel shifted into Park and rubbed her temples. After a moment, she exited the car, glanced down the block, and said a silent prayer of gratitude. The street was empty of nosy neighbors who would only be too happy to tell her how to handle the situation. She opened the back door. "Hey, Sweetie."

"No. Don't talk to me," Kansas wailed. With a blotchy face and piercing sobs, she exited the car.

"Shh." Mel rushed to the front door. Fumbling with the lock, she set her purse down. "Come on. We'll figure something out." She pushed open the door and sighed when she saw Kansas running towards her.

Seeing Kansas stoop to grab her purse, she smiled, pride expanding Mel's chest. *She's so thoughtful.*

"I'm calling my mom." She jogged past Mel with the purse and slammed her bedroom door. "She'll let me have friends over."

The last thing I want is Kansas calling Opal in Kuwait, sobbing about an overnight. "Okay." Mel took a deep breath and tried to remove all emotion from her words. "You can have Alyssa and McKenzie over. But next time, you ask me before inviting friends over, do you understand?" She hated appearing weak, but she also wanted to protect Opal from undue stress.

The door opened, and Kansas stepped out holding the purse. "I will. I promise." She swiped a handful of dark curls from her eyes and smeared her runny nose with both hands. "Can we have pizza at my party?"

That's all I need: a repeat of last weekend, calling

parents to pick up sick kids. "I'll think about it."

"Thanks, Auntie." She wound her arms around Mel's legs. "We don't have to eat pizza. The last time I ate pizza, I had a stomachache."

She ruffled her curls as she prepared a new to-do list. Lawn service by Saturday, search for ways to keep kids busy, and grocery shop. They walked into the kitchen, with neon-yellow walls, harvest-yellow flooring, countertops from the seventies, and updated stainless-steel appliances.

"I'm thirsty." Kansas opened the refrigerator.

"Drink only one juice box." Mel searched the cupboards for instant macaroni and cheese. The meal took three minutes to prepare, but the box failed to mention the time required for a child to eat the meal.

After fifteen minutes, Kansas had only rearranged the bright-orange noodles in the cup.

"Would you rather have a hot dog?"

She nodded.

Mel placed two hot dogs in the microwave and two white buns on a plate. She remembered the salad Clay ordered and the photo of him as a child. Guilt crept from her gut. *I should feed Kansas a rainbow of colors at mealtime. Tomorrow, I will call the yard service company and go grocery shopping for healthier food options.*

"Can we go to the park?" Kansas stuffed the last of her hot dog into her mouth. "I'm done."

"Sure, let me grab my laptop first." Mel stepped outside and tilted her face to the sun. She loved early summer because everything stayed light until nine o'clock. At the end of the street, she held Kansas' hand and turned left onto the walking path, stepping under the bright, sea-green canopy of treetops.

Mel loved the miles of walking and bike paths in her neighborhood, but until Kansas came to stay, she rarely used them. The park was small but had enough green space for picnic tables, a dozen swings, three slides, and climbing bars.

All the locals called this area Triangle Park, not because of the shape, but because all three paths met in this open field. Mel sat at a vacant picnic table and watched Kansas run toward the swings. After opening her laptop, she had difficulty focusing on the screen. Her thoughts drifted over the events of the day and the things she needed to accomplish.

"Hello."

Clay's familiar scent of cedar and citrus drifted from behind her. She smiled and turned.

"Mind if I sit down?"

The timber of his voice sent shivers up her spine. "No, not at all." She closed her laptop and swung her legs around.

"Which one is yours?"

"Auntie, push me," Kansas called from a swing. Her legs kicked in midair. "Please?"

"The one needing help." Mel stood and waved for Clay to follow her for thirty steps. "Kansas, this is Clayton, my friend from work."

He held out his right hand. "Hello, Kansas."

She gave two of his nail-bitten fingers a quick shake. "Are you a good pusher?"

"I can do it." Mel grabbed the chains. She wrestled Kansas back and let go.

The swing swayed. "No, higher," Kansas said. "Please, Auntie, try harder."

He stepped closer. "Mind if I try?"

"Go ahead." Mel shrugged.

"I'm the best pusher in Rockerville." He flexed both arms.

Kansas giggled.

Back at the picnic table, Mel didn't open her computer. Instead, she held her breath as Clay sent Kansas high into the air.

"Higher," she shrieked.

"Okay, hang on tight." Clay pushed harder.

After seeing Kansas remain in her swing, Mel exhaled. She softened her gaze. *They're both so cute: thick, dark curls, brown eyes, and a dimple.* Mel guessed Clay was Opal's age, but so were a million other men, and half had brown eyes and dark hair. She reminded herself of the incident with Kansas' kindergarten teacher. He and Kansas had similar features. Mel'd drilled her sister about him.

Opal laughed and joked about believing what you wanted to believe.

Kansas squealed.

She had never seen a child go higher on a swing. Mel tensed. Would he send her over the top? When the swing finally stopped, she slumped against the table.

"Wanna play tag?" Kansas slapped Clay's thigh. "You're it."

He ran after her.

Moments later, five kids shouted and ran everywhere.

Mel could feel her chest tighten with happiness and sadness—the all-American dream. Mom, Dad, and their kids at the park after dinner and then putting them to bed. She dreamt of being part of a fictional family like those portrayed on TV and in books but ended up with dysfunction. Her dad hated anything outdoors. He disliked noise, social gatherings, animals, and probably kids. Her mom was a nurse on the second shift and flashed her biggest smile when leaving for work.

She wasn't much older than Kansas when she figured out the best way to deal with her father's moodiness was to be away from the house. She found refuge at the library, and when Opal was big enough to sit in the stroller, she took her along. And now she was the caretaker for Opal's daughter. Would Kansas remember these trips to the park as a happy childhood memory?

"Auntie." Kansas scrambled onto the picnic table, her face flushed from running. "I had fun."

"Me, too." Clay stood at the edge of the table. "Next time, your aunt will have to join us."

"She's too old and always has work to do." Kansas giggled.

I'm forty-one, not seventy-one. No wonder Opal and Paula pester me. But I also have a career to manage besides chauffeuring, cooking, and cleaning. Always being responsible is hard. She reached over and tickled Kansas. "If I didn't work, I couldn't buy you new clothes and toys."

"I know, Auntie. Could you buy me something to make me strong like him?" She flexed her right arm like Clay had earlier.

He laughed. "Muscles come from eating right, doing homework, chores, and going to bed on time."

"You're funny." Kansas batted her eyelashes.

Did she wish she had an Uncle Clay instead of an Auntie? "Hey, kiddo." Mel stood. "I'd better get you home. You still need a bath, and we forgot to check your backpack for homework."

"I don't want to go." She folded her little arms across her chest.

"Only good listeners get to have sleepovers." Mel used her only leverage and hoped Clay wouldn't have to witness a meltdown.

"Okay." She grinned. "We can go, but when my mom comes home, we'll have a giant sleepover, and he can come. Okay?" She placed a small hand on his forearm. "My mom will like you."

"Sounds like fun," he said. "Come on. I'll escort you back to your home."

Kansas chatted the entire way with stories about the boys in her class being messy and talking without raising their hands.

Mel didn't realize so much drama happened in first grade. After turning the corner, she swallowed hard. *I own the ugliest house on the block.* The paint around the windows had peeled off, two of her bushes had died, the weeds had grown out of control, and the grass needed mowing. She slowed her steps and glanced up at his expression. He didn't look shocked. "I forgot to send the lawn service a check, and they dropped me." She shrugged. "The lawnmower's buried somewhere in the garage, probably between my sister's storage boxes and my late husband's things. The inside is nicer, a little outdated, but clean. Can I offer you a cold drink?"

"I can make you a root beer float." Kansas grabbed his left hand.

"I'd love one," he said.

If he hated root beer, he'd still drink it. Mel half grinned. *I'll have to remember to be out of town if Opal*

48

deploys when Kansas is a teenager. She walked through the front door and motioned for Clay to follow her down the hall and into the kitchen.

"This is a bright-yellow." He pointed to the walls.

Mel chuckled. "I know. Shortly after my husband died, my sister and Kansas surprised me by painting the kitchen. Guess who picked the color?"

"My mom can fix and do anything." Kansas beamed.

"Nice. I can't wait to meet her. She sounds amazing."

Mel put the soda pop and ice cream on the island. "I'll make the floats. Kansas, you check your backpack for homework."

"I finished my homework at day care, but I'll check."

"Grab a chair, Clay." She motioned to a bar stool.

"I'm not much of a soda guy, so make mine small."

She slid three floats along the counter.

"Homework is all done." Kansas dragged her chair closer to Clay.

He took a small sip of the root beer float and smacked his lips. "Delicious."

Kansas mimicked his movements. "Delicious."

He's not fancy, but something about him makes me happy to be single. Mel scooped a big spoonful of ice cream from her cup onto her tongue as she studied him. The creamy ice cream tasted delicious but was a poor substitute when longing for a kiss. *Will I ever have another kiss?*

"Ever see a microwave?" Clay grinned.

"Yeah." Kansas pointed above the stove.

He shook his head and barely waved the tip of his

pinky finger.

Mel groaned. "That was the worst dad joke."

Kansas' fake laugh filled the area. "That was funny." She slapped the table.

After exchanging a glance with Clay, Mel laughed. For thirty minutes, she sat, pretending they were the perfect family. But like all good things, the fantasy had to end. "Come on, kiddo. Time for bed."

With heavy sighs, Kansas walked with Mel to the door to say good night.

"I had the best time." Kansas ignored Clay's outstretched hand and wrapped her arms around his neck. "When can you come over again?"

"Better ask your aunt." He stood and swung her around.

Mel hovered in the doorway. She had an odd ache in her arms and chest. *Crazy. I don't know if I'm coming down with something or just want to be in his embrace.*

He set Kansas down, turned, and winked.

"Come on, kiddo." Mel gave a limp wave and nudged the door closed with her shoulder. "Bath time and then bed." Twenty minutes later, Mel tucked the bedcovers around her sleeping niece. She stepped from the room, debating about reading the remodeling contract or contacting the mowing service but instead emailed Opal. She couldn't wait to tell her sister about the pride in Kansas' voice when she told people her mom could fix and do anything.

Chapter Six

On Tuesday, Mel dropped Kansas at child care and swung by Coffee King before heading to the office. As she drove, she inhaled the aroma of freshly brewed coffee. *The only thing better than the smell of coffee is the scent of Clay.* When she walked into the office, she laid a cup of coffee and a wrapped protein breakfast sandwich on Paula's desk.

She leaned in and sniffed the wrapper. "Bacon. My favorite. Any special reason? Not that you need one for the best administrative assistant. Maybe this is a small token of appreciation because I predicted Mr. Tall, Dark, and Handsome..."

Without waiting for Paula to finish, she smiled and sauntered down the hall. *Let her wonder if I have a secret, exciting life.* Seated in front of the monitors, she let her thoughts wander back to Clay. Would another kiss thrill her? Or have her making excuses because she didn't want to see him?

That afternoon, Paula didn't have to remind her to shut off her computer. Today, she couldn't stop watching the clock, and instead of time flying, the minutes and hours dragged their arms across the clock's face. She stuffed her laptop into her bag. *Tomorrow, no more thinking about Clay and the kiss. And I will exercise and only eat non-processed foods.* Mel paused at Paula's desk. "This doesn't happen often. Me, leaving before you."

"Boss Lady, hold the elevator. I'll be right there."

"Sure thing." Mel strolled to the elevator and waited a moment before hitting the up arrow.

Paula arrived breathless as the door opened. "So, what's his flaw?" She leaned closer as the door shut. "You can tell me."

"Huh." Mel watched the doors close. The elevator rumbled and ascended a flight.

"No guy's perfect." Paula placed her hands on her hips.

Mel shrugged. "I haven't known him too long, but he bites his nails." She stepped through the open elevator doors into the lobby.

"Nail-biter." Paula tapped her chin and made a lot of hmmm sounds.

"Is that a deal-breaker?" Mel leaned closer as they walked through the parking lot.

"When Clay bites his fingernails, do you cringe and want to poke out your eye?"

She paused. The last time Clay's finger brushed his bottom lip all she could think about was her thumb on his lips. Would he playfully bite the pad of her thumb? Heat soared from the core of her being. Mel resisted the urge to fan her face. "Of course not."

"So, what do you think?"

Mel tilted her head. "I think he's nervous." *And I'm falling for him.*

"That's good." Paula clapped. "If you find his faults endearing, no problem. But if his habits are cringeworthy, run."

"Wow. You are the best administrative assistant."

"I know." Paula turned and sashayed toward her

car. "Any more advice, it'll cost you. I do work for food."

She smiled and resisted the urge to wrap her arms around her waist. *I find Clay endearing. Will I see him tonight?*

****

Mel walked into the day care, found the sign-out sheet, and jotted down her name and pickup time, wondering if Clay had other flaws. She shook her head. *Kansas and work are my priorities.* She sighed, and because of Leo, the executive manager who volunteered her to cover for Bill, she had added Bill's direct reports to her list of concerns.

"Auntie, you're here." Kansas raced forward, dragging her jacket and backpack. Her small fingers tugged Mel to the door. "Come on."

At the car, Mel watched her scramble inside.

"What day is it?"

Mel checked the buckle on her booster seat. "Tuesday, and aren't you a little young to forget what day it is?"

She shook her head. "I had a long day. How many days until my overnight?"

"Four." Mel slipped behind the wheel and shifted into gear. "So, tell me about your day."

Kansas had no trouble describing the classroom drama.

When she turned onto Fourth Street, she sucked in a breath, her gaze widening. The pink crabapple trees and lavender lilac bushes had blossomed. She lowered the car windows. "Smells like summer."

"Sure does, Auntie."

Mel smiled at seeing flower gardens and ceramic

planters bursting with life on her neighbors' steps. *On Sunday, I'm buying flowers, too.* She drove into her driveway, and her thoughts shifted back to work. *Did I email Bill's team about ordering bath tissue?* She slipped out of the front seat.

"Look, Auntie." Kansas yanked on her right arm. "Everything is so pretty."

Mel squinted and glanced at the house numbers. This was her house, but everything looked new and fresh. She expanded her lungs as the tension in her muscles lessened, a feeling of excitement and peace settling over her. "Ahh." Slipped from her lips. No one had ever gone out of their way to do something so sweet and kind. Two giant planters bursting with deep shades of red, navy-blue, and white flowers bordered her walkway. Green flowering bushes replaced the dead, decaying shrubs, and the smell of fresh-cut grass penetrated the air.

"Auntie, take my picture." Kansas posed in front of the flowers. "Send them all to my mom. Okay?"

"Sure, kiddo. But could we get one picture with you not sticking out your tongue?"

She smiled.

Mel snapped a few more photos, capturing the moment right before the kid's tongue came back out. She shook her head—a six-year-old's sense of humor. Before entering the house, she scrolled through the photos and sent one to Clay.

—*My yard looks beautiful. I am at a loss for words and can't stop grinning. Thank you.*—

****

For the rest of the week, Mel brought Kansas to the park in the evenings without her laptop. She tried to balance work and home, but instead of finding a happy medium, she experienced guilt. Some employees' questions stayed unanswered for days, but Mel refused to regret standing in the playground with the sunlight fading in the west.

"Higher, Auntie."

"One second." Mel shook out her achy arms. "This time, you'll hit the sky."

She giggled. "Nope, not as high."

Twice, Clay jogged past.

She waved like paparazzi spotting a Hollywood celebrity.

He slowed long enough to give Kansas a few pushes and Mel a wink.

After briefly interacting with Clay, she felt warmth spreading through her body like butter over corn on the cob.

"Thanks, Uncle," Kansas called from her airborne swing.

Mel blushed at Kansas' familiarity. The only uncle Kansas knew was married to Mel. She opened her mouth and then pressed her lips tightly together. What could she say to explain?

He jogged backward for a dozen steps. "Bye, Kansas. Bye, Auntie."

I need to stop worrying about Kansas offending him. Mel sighed. *And start thinking about this weekend. Will we kiss? Should I carry breath mints?*

****

On Thursday night, Kansas informed her she had invited a few more friends to the overnight. Sighing, she tucked Kansas into bed before heading to her spare bedroom to catch up on work correspondence. But before logging into her company account, she spotted an email from Opal. She sucked in air as the hammering of her heart pounded against her rib cage. Did Opal sustain an injury? Did her deployment get extended?

She clicked to read Opal's letter and let out a vast sigh. She wrote to say she missed everyone and liked the photos.

Opal, can someone fall in love in a week? OMG, this man cleaned up my entire yard and dropped off huge planters filled with flowers the color of the MN Twinkles. I think about him all the time. Is this just hormonal? Kansas is, of course, doing well. She has no trouble making friends. We read every night, and she still holds my hand whenever we walk through parking lots. Kansas calls my new friend from work Uncle because he can push her high on the swings. We bumped into him a few times in the park. Stay safe. We both miss you. Love always, Melody.

****

At work on Friday, Mel stared at the computer monitors on her workstation and tried to concentrate. Her thoughts shifted to Saturday. *Clay. Girls. Lots of six-year-old girls.* She pushed back from the desk and rubbed the knot in her neck. *Clay on the sofa beside me. Kansas asking about the time, opening the door, adding guests, snacks, games, door-to-dash entrée requests, and begging for party favors.* The knot found its way to her stomach.

I need to tell him Saturday won't work. Mel sighed. *It's for the best. In a couple of months, Opal will be home, and then if he's still interested...* She leaned back, easing the tightness in her chest. Slowly, she hammered out a message.

—Clay, I need to cancel my invitation. Kansas invited friends for a sleepover. It's my first time hosting, and I'm imagining all the worst-case scenarios.—

Seconds later, Clay responded.

—I have hosted a couple of sleepovers for my godchild. Do you want some help?—

She let out a pent-up breath and raced to reply.

—Yes, do you have any ideas on how to entertain them? Kansas isn't the type to sit and watch movies all night, and I couldn't find a single bouncy house for rent.—

—I can come over with my tent and some wood. The girls can have a sleepover in the backyard. And I can teach them how to make dinner over a campfire.—

She pursed her lips as she typed a response.

—A fire with five girls? Someone's hair will catch fire, or the tent will blow away.—

—Trust me. The kids won't burn, and the tent won't take flight.—

Mel sucked on her bottom lip. *Do I have a choice?*

—Okay, I will trust you. And before I forget, thank you. You don't know how much I appreciate your help.—

—Don't be so fast to thank me. I'm only helping because of your sports package. I am hoping you have the football package, too. LOL. Regardless, I'll be over on Saturday at one. I still plan to watch the game.—

The exchange of texts helped Mel refocus on work, and when she heard Paula walk into her office jiggling keys, she looked at the clock twice. "Five o'clock, already. The day flew by." She shut down her computer. "What would I do without you?"

"Well, you could ask Mr. Tall, Dark, and Handsome if he has any single friends or a brother."

"I'll keep that in mind." Mel followed Paula into the elevator. "You still haven't found a fellow dog lover at the shelter or Mr. Buff at the gym?"

She shook her head. "Lots, but they all seem to break my number one rule."

"What's that?"

"They have to behave better than the canines, or they can't look better in spandex than me." Paula laughed.

Mel walked into the parking lot, shaking the visual out of her head. She scanned the lot, hoping to glimpse Clay's truck. He must have left at three with the rest of his crew.

After picking up Kansas, Mel dismissed the idea of grocery shopping and headed straight home. She wanted to ask Clay what he needed for the campfire dinner. Of course, she'd have to text him again. *I hope he finds my questions endearing and not annoying.*

At home, Mel exchanged half a dozen texts with Clay, keeping Kansas in the dark to avoid a million questions and an epic battle to get her to sleep.

Mel sent Kansas to bed a little before nine, but after three bedtime stories and two glasses of water, she still needed to rub her back before she fell asleep. At ten o'clock, Mel tiptoed out of the bedroom and down the hall.

I can't even get one kid to sleep. How will I manage five?

****

On Saturday, Mel awoke to Kansas tugging on her

pillow.

"Auntie, get up."

Mel didn't have to check the clock to know the sun hadn't risen. She flipped open the comforter. "Thirty more minutes, and we'll…"

Kansas leaped onto the bed.

Oof. Mel huffed. "Get off of me, you bed hog." She lovingly rolled Kansas to the far side.

Kansas grunted and laid her head on the spare pillow.

Mel closed her eyes. An hour later, she woke up and got dressed. "Hurry, Kansas, we have lots to do. I need to clean the house. You need to put away all your toys and make your bed."

At one, Clay arrived and reviewed Mel's list. He added bubbles, balls, and jump ropes.

Mel winked. "If they don't behave, we can tie them up."

"Auntie. That's not nice."

She ruffled her niece's hair. "You're right, but I was only joking."

"If you're not good, we can tie you up." Kansas laughed.

"Ha, ha." Mel chuckled. "My biggest fear is a gang of six-year-olds tying up Auntie."

Clay waved at the door. "You two better be off. I have a game to watch."

A few hours later, Mel and Kansas returned with so much food. Mel made three trips to the car hauling everything. Just as she finished, the first guest arrived, followed by a convoy of three more.

Two moms didn't want to leave their daughters overnight and said they'd be back at nine.

Alyssa's mom thanked Mel over fifteen times.

Is Alyssa a handful, or did her mom just need me time?

"Come on, everyone." Kansas waved an arm and started toward the backyard. She turned every twenty steps to ensure all four girls and Clay trailed after her.

Mel also followed, keeping her gaze on the potential stragglers.

The chatter of five little girls mingled with the distant weekend sounds of mowers, birds chirping, and dogs barking.

"What is this?" Mel turned toward Clay and pointed to a ten-person tent, a collapsible picnic table, a stone block firepit, and lights strung along the wooden fence. "Wow."

The girls squealed and ran like a pack of wild dogs.

"How?" She moved closer to Clay. "When did you get this all done? We were only gone for two hours."

His face lit up with a toothy smile.

"You did all this?"

The tip of his shoe pushed against the grass as he grinned. "I'm certain you signed off on remodeling your backyard with Bill's contract." He winked.

"This is awesome." She wanted to wrap her arms around him as she planted kisses on his face. Instead, she grabbed his right hand and squeezed it before letting go. "I can't believe what you've done. Did you get to see any of the game?"

"A little." His smile twisted. "I caught most of the commentary and scores on my earbuds."

"Uncle." Kansas tugged on his right arm. "What do we do with our packs and stuff?"

He lifted the tent flap. "Sleeping bags and

backpacks in here."

The girls raced to the door, their bags dragging and beating against each other.

"Okay." Clay bit the nail on his ring finger.

He's nervous. Mel softened her gaze. "How can I help?"

"First, we have to go over fire safety rules, and then we will play games for prizes."

Mel watched the girls try to get his attention and stepped beside him, offering moral support from the shirt-tugging, question-asking mob of curious girls. Would any of the girls call him Uncle by night's end?

He explained how the fire had to stay in the firepit, and only the adults could add wood. Next, he explained the rules for the races.

Alyssa won a small camp chair for the most jumping jacks.

"Line up." Clay pointed toward a spot alongside the fence. "Relay race with stuffed animals."

One girl pouted. "I didn't bring a teddy."

Mel started for the house. "Kansas has extras. I'll run inside."

"It's okay." Clay held up four neck pillows. "We'll run the race with these."

The girls giggled and ran with *Construction Dunn Wright* pillows wrapped around their heads, like earmuffs on a cold winter day.

Animal trivia and a spelling bee wound up the games. All the girls won flashlights, compasses, and small collapsible camp stools with company logos imprinted on the prizes.

Clay motioned the girls closer. "After dinner, we'll play animal bingo for the rest of the prizes."

Mel overheard a girl tell Kansas she had a cool uncle. *Could I get Clay to be my cool boyfriend?*

Chapter Seven

Mel stood in the backyard, listening to the sound of the burning logs crackle. She watched Clay demonstrate how to add vegetables and seasoning to their chicken foil packet. Then he showed the girls how to seal the tinfoil to steam the food.

The girls clapped as he used big mitts and tongs to place the food on the glowing amber coals, but then they became restless.

"Auntie, can we use your phone to take pictures?"

Mel handed over her phone and watched the girls pose and giggle for thirty minutes. "Good thing it's a new phone, and I have a ton of memory." She moved closer to the fire and sniffed. "Everything smells so good. When can we eat?"

"Soon." Clay began retrieving the hot foil meals. "We need to release the steam before the girls sit to eat."

After opening the packets, Mel placed the contents on individual paper plates before rushing back into the house for the containers of salads and bread. With the table laden with food and the girls poised to eat, she snapped a few photos.

"Rub a dub dub." Clay rubbed his stomach. "Let's eat this grub."

The girls giggled and mimicked his actions.

Mel snagged a seat next to Clay. She stabbed at the

chicken, and instead of the plastic tines on the fork breaking, they slipped into the tender chunk of meat. After the first few bites, she paused. "Amazing, moist, and delicious." She stole a glance at Clay, and she could see pride beaming from his smile.

The girls echoed her appreciation with lip-smacking sounds, and after dinner, they played animal bingo.

Clay sat next to Mel by the fire.

She let out a slow breath. "I can't believe we didn't have to tie the kids up. Thank you."

"No, thank you. I miss this. I used to have my godson and his friends over for sleepovers, but Brenda ended my visits." He sucked in his top and bottom lip as he stared into the fire. He sighed. "Well, I don't have to tell you why. You've met her—"

"Why do adults act like spoiled toddlers? I'm sure he misses having you in his life. We haven't known each other long, but I can't imagine telling Kansas you couldn't return."

"Thank you." He smiled. "And she's adorable."

"Although you have not seen her when she is tired or things don't go her way. You know, viral tantrums. But you're right, she is very lovable. I don't know what I would do if Kansas and my sister weren't in my life." She watched him gaze into the fire. *Helpful, kind, good-looking...why would any woman leave him at the altar?* With the question on the tip of her tongue, she pondered how to best ask the question. She didn't want to pry, but she needed to know if he had a drug, alcohol, or gambling problem.

The girls rushed from the tent, chanting, "S'mores, please."

Clay rose effortlessly from the ground and handed out sticks. "Everyone stays seated on their bottoms, and only the stick tips and marshmallows go into the fire."

After forty-five minutes of sticky goo, Mel realized the girls didn't want to eat the marshmallows. They only wanted to play with the fire. She glanced at Clay and mouthed the word, *help*.

He tapped an index finger to his chin.

She raised her eyebrows. *He can't be out of ideas.* "Girls, want to get ready for bed?"

"No," voices echoed across the fire in surround sound as each girl shook her head.

Clay covered his widening grin with a hand and winked.

Is he teasing me? Mel narrowed her gaze.

He pointed to the tent. "Who wants to make shadow puppets?"

The girls tossed their sticks into the fire and retreated to the tent.

Clay crawled inside and demonstrated with his flashlight and hands.

The girls rewarded his efforts with a chorus of giggles.

Just after sunset, a mom arrived for two of the girls.

Mel and Kansas walked them to the driveway.

"Thanks for inviting us," the girls shouted.

Mel nudged Kansas.

"Thanks for coming." Kansas tugged at her right hand. "Hurry, Auntie, I want to go back."

Trailing a step behind, she rounded the corner to the backyard and watched Clay add three logs to the fire. She sat with the remaining girls and listened to stories about unicorns and fairies. As the flames grew brighter, Mel gave a long, loud yawn.

Soon, all the girls yawned.

Clay placed two adult sleeping bags between the tent's entrance and the fire.

"Are you staying?" Kansas stepped closer.

"Only until the fire burns down," Clay said.

Kansas squatted and patted the bag. "Can you stay all night?"

"Yeah, stay all night?" Alyssa echoed.

"Sure, I will." He folded his legs and plopped down onto the bag. "Nothing better than sleeping on the ground."

Kansas giggled. "Auntie, will you sleep outside, too?"

"No, I'll sleep in the tent with you. Unless..."— she clapped—"you'd rather sleep in the big house. We could watch a movie." Her voice ended on a higher, wistful note.

The girls shined their flashlights on Mel. "No, no, no."

"Okay, crawl into your sleeping bags and turn off your lights." Mel sat next to Clay on the sleeping bag and talked in a low whisper until she heard the first sound of a tiny snore.

"Is Kansas' dad in the military, too?" Clay asked.

Mel shrugged. "My sister never mentions the father."

"Did you ever ask?"

"Of course. She said, 'They were two ships passing at night, and she has no regrets.' "

He pursed his lips and drew his eyebrows closer together. He shook his head. "Didn't he want to be a part of her life?"

"I don't know. But I know my sister is a wonderful mother and an officer in the Army Reserve. She takes care of her soldiers, and when not deployed, she helps people live their best life."

"Sorry." He brushed his index finger across his lower lip before folding his hands into his lap. "I didn't mean to imply anything. Kansas is a wonderful kid, so I know her mom must be amazing, too." He poked the fire with a stick, and the orange coals glowed brighter. "I hear Bill is coming back on Wednesday."

Mel clapped. "I know. I'm so ready to be done with his job."

"Was working with me so awful?"

She imagined he resembled the pound puppies at Paula's volunteer gig. She shook her head and brushed a hand against his left bicep. "No, you were the only good thing about covering for him. The man has more meetings than anyone I know, and my emails have tripled."

"Well, I'm glad to hear I wasn't a problem. I enjoy being with you. I'd like to see you again."

Mel dropped her arms back into her lap, appearing calm and collected while her insides danced happily. *He wants to see me!* "Well, yes, I'd like that."

He stood and stirred the fire with the poker. The logs sparked, and the flames grew. He turned and plopped onto the ground.

Their knees touched, and she could feel her insides turning soft and toasty like a marshmallow. She shifted, wishing they were sitting in tiny camp chairs instead of the hard ground.

"If you don't mind me asking, how come you and

your husband never had kids?"

She smiled as she considered the best way to respond. *Most people didn't understand when I got married, I lacked the inner strength to voice my opinions and found life more manageable when I agreed.* She inhaled deeply. "I really liked Harold. He was kind, and I enjoyed listening to him talk about his day and found his point of view interesting. After we became serious, he told me he didn't want kids or even a dog."

"And what did you want?"

"I had a turbulent childhood, and I guess I wanted safety. We loved each other, and we were happy. So, yes, more than okay. But if I met Harold today, I'm not sure he'd be enough." The warmth from his knee resting on her leg sparked long-forgotten feelings. She wanted to dance beside the flames, welcome the heat, and leap into the ring of fire or his arms.

Clay moved to his knees, leaned forward, and stirred the embers. The flames grew tall, licking the night sky before he settled back to sitting beside her on the sleeping bag. "Is that why you don't have any family photos in your house?"

"No, nothing so dramatic." She laughed. "My real estate agent requested I take down anything personal. So, I removed all the photos. Then before we listed the house, my sister found out about her deployment. We had a mad dash packing and moving all her things to storage or my garage." She shrugged. "Now, I'm getting Kansas to day care and me to work each day." She tapped a finger against his forearm. "So, my turn. Did you really get left at the altar?"

He leaned closer. "Yes."

"Want to tell me about it?"

"Not much to tell." He stretched his arms behind him and leaned back. "Liz and I were high school sweethearts. We both graduated from college. I started working at my dad's accounting firm, and we started planning our wedding. But instead of feeling happy, I griped and complained. My grandma's health failed, and she kept telling me to live my life with no regrets."

Clay drew his knees to his chest and wrapped his arms around his legs. "Two weeks before the wedding, I told Liz I quit working for my dad. She joked about me having wedding jitters. Later, she claimed I had a fear of growing up. We fought a lot. I knew we shouldn't get married. But instead of telling her, I arrived in my tuxedo, and she didn't show up."

"I'm so sorry. I can't even imagine." Mel drew her eyebrows together and studied Clay. *At least it wasn't drugs or drinking, but why wouldn't he talk to her? I lack backbone, but I think I'd at least talk it through.* "Why didn't you go see her?"

He chewed on his thumbnail and stared into the fire.

The flames danced over the red, pulsing embers, and a night owl serenaded them with questions. *"Hoo-hoo-hoo."*

Mel stretched out her legs and wiggled her toes closer to the fire. She tried to imagine her reaction if someone she loved didn't attend a special event. *I'd confront them.* She clenched her fists. *Is he afraid to fight? If things sour between us, will he ghost me?* She drew her toasty toes closer and crossed her legs. "Did you like working with your dad? I know I wouldn't have been able to work with my dad, and as much as I like my sister, we still couldn't run a business together."

Clay unfolded his legs, their knees once again touching. "For six months, he nitpicked and second-guessed me. He spent all his time checking over my work. I loved my dad, but he made a lousy boss."

"Maybe you didn't enjoy being an accountant?"

"I enjoyed accounting, summarizing, and reporting. I am a numbers guy."

"Do you think Liz had a point about you not wanting to grow up?" Mel rubbed her chin. "Or maybe you fear confrontation."

"Whoa." He raked his right hand through his hair. "Let me guess, you have a college degree in psychology."

"Computer science, but Harold was a psychologist. Maybe some of him wore off on me." She weaved her fingers through his as the crackling fire cast shadows on low-hanging branches hovering over the tent. Mel leaned closer.

Clay released her hand and wrapped an arm around her.

The strength of his arms comforted and excited her simultaneously. She drew her left arm across his lower back.

He lowered his head and kissed her lips.

Her senses became one warm rush, fueling her pounding heart.

Clay placed soft kisses from the base of her neck to the lobes of her ears.

She gripped his shirt, not knowing what to do with the tidal wave of emotion. Desire surged along with fear, making her skin tingle and her palms sweat. *What if I'm a terrible kisser? How do I know if I'm doing this right? It's been so long. Oh my. Did he moan?* "Clay," she breathed. "Yes, Clay."

His hands traveled from her waist to the back of her shoulders. He eased her onto his sleeping bag. He planted a kiss below the pulse point on her neck.

She moaned and inched her trembling hands across his tight abs. Cool night air replaced his lips, and she opened her eyes.

He squeezed her hand and nodded toward the tent.

Mel heard someone mumble.

"You should go." He exhaled.

The passion in his eyes and the heat from his kisses slowed her response. She flirted with staying outside. "I don't want to leave."

"Please," he pleaded.

After one last kiss, she grabbed her sleeping bag and left him with the dying embers. Inside the tent, she closed her eyes and imagined a different ending to the night.

****

On Sunday morning, the sun flashed through the tent flap. Mel sat up, ran her fingers through her hair, and counted the sleeping girls. She exhaled. *All present and accounted for.* She stretched, testing out her back and legs before slipping from the tent.

Clay glanced up from shoveling ash into a metal bucket. "How are you this fine morning?"

Heat crept up her neck, and she dropped her gaze to the ground. "Refreshed, except for a certain ache."

He leaned the shovel against a chair and stepped closer. "Me, too." His lips brushed her cheek. "I had a wonderful night, thank you."

"Auntie, I'm hungry," Kansas called out, crawling from the tent.

Mel jumped away from Clay, clasping her hands together. *Did Kansas see or hear anything?*

"Uncle, you stayed."

"Of course. How about we go inside and make some pancakes?"

Does he feel obligated? Mel tugged the hem of her shirt. *I feel like I'm taking advantage of him.* "You've already helped so much. The girls can eat cereal and milk."

He winked. "What if I want to stay?"

"Well." She tried to pull her lips together as she flashed her teeth in a big, toothy grin. *Why am I a lovesick teenager around him? This is all moving so fast. Yet everything feels so right. Even my gut says this is the guy for me.* "If you're sure, then you can cook."

Kansas tugged his right hand. "My mom makes chocolate chip pancakes."

He clapped his hands. "Those are my specialty."

The best night is turning into the best day. I might have to ask Paula to babysit so I can spend some adult time with him. She wrapped her arms around her waist and squeezed. *Is he for real? If this is a dream, I hope I don't wake up for another few hours.*

After eating, the girls packed their things to wait for their parents.

At nine o'clock, Alyssa's mom called to say she was running late and could return the favor by taking Kansas for a few hours this afternoon.

Clay stood near enough to hear both sides of the conversation. He gave Mel a slight smile and winked.

I don't think he's winking because he wants to

watch the game. She swallowed. This was what she wanted last night, but in the middle of the day, she was no longer certain it was a good idea. *He'll see my wrinkles and droopy skin. I haven't had a pedicure.*

"Make yourself coffee while the girls and I wash dishes."

Mel nodded and walked over to the coffee machine. *At least, I won't have to worry about falling asleep. Between the caffeine and nervous jitters, I'll be lucky if I can sleep at all this week.*

An hour later, Alyssa's mom swung by and mentioned she'd return around one to pick up Kansas and take them to a church carnival close to the house.

Kansas and Alyssa hugged good-bye. "I'll miss you," they echoed.

"So, you're free this afternoon?" Clay leaned close, his words a whisper.

Mel could feel the heat radiating from his body. Instead of smelling citrus and cedar, she inhaled the remnants from last night's campfire and this morning's pancakes. Instead of his scent coming from a bottle, it came from the memories they made together. *She repressed the desire to pull him closer. They shared the same scent.* She raised an eyebrow. "And…"

"I believe the game starts at one."

"Are you watching baseball?" Kansas stuck out her tongue. "Yuk. Boring."

Mel blushed. "Lots of baseball." After helping Clay load the tent into his truck, she stood waving good-bye. Mel's thoughts trailed after him until she caught a glance at the time. *Two and a half hours before the game. Where do I start? Clean sheets.* "Come on, kiddo, I've got work to do." She hustled

Kansas toward the house.

"Auntie…"

"Sure." Mel stood in the kitchen. "Wait, what?"

"Can I look at the pictures we took on the phone?" Kansas repeated.

Mel let out a sigh. *Thank God, I agreed to let her search for photos and not have another sleepover.* In the bedroom, she placed clean, crisp sheets onto the queen-size bed and spritzed the pillows with perfume. She sniffed the first notes of pear and pineapple, which faded to vanilla. *Will our scents mingle or clash?* She fanned her cheeks with both hands as her thoughts warmed her blood. After checking on Kansas, she jumped into the shower with her razor. She wasn't sure what everyone shaved these days, but she didn't want to look like Big Foot if their game went into extra innings. She adjusted the water cooler. *Will I score?*

Chapter Eight

Sunday afternoon, Mel again stood in the entryway, but instead of waving good-bye to Kansas and Alyssa, she greeted Clay. The sight of him shifting his weight from foot to foot, holding a handful of daisies and baby's breath, took her breath away. "For me?" She batted her lashes and motioned for him to come inside.

"Fresh from Abby's grocery."

Mel buried her nose in the bundle of blooms. "My favorite flowers. How did you know?" She walked into the kitchen, hoping he wouldn't notice the slight tremble in her hands. After grabbing a tall glass from the cupboard, she arranged the flowers.

"They smell inviting." He swooped Mel into an embrace.

Her feet dangled off the ground.

"But you're my favorite flower…intoxicating."

A flush of warmth radiated through her as the fluttering of her heart pattered against his chest.

He eased her to the floor and waltzed her into the living room.

In a hurry to feel his lips, she jerked her head forward and connected with his nose. She swallowed and leaned back, feeling like she had two left arms, two left feet, and a million overactive sweat glands. "I don't know," she stammered.

He clasped her shoulders with his hands and pulled her forward, brushing his lips against her forehead. "I'm nervous, too."

After placing her hands on his hips, she shifted to his upper back. *Did I brush my teeth?* Certain sweat was beading on her upper lip, she staggered back. Nothing felt right. With her gaze fixed on the floor, she cleared her throat. "Do you want to watch the game?"

"Mel." He tipped her chin with a thumb. "Of course, I enjoy being with you. We can watch a game, go for a walk, whatever..." His thumb lingered on her lower lip. "I want you to be honest. If we're moving too fast, just say so. I like you."

"Thank you." She tugged him onto the sofa, and within minutes, the Twinkles and Royaltons were playing. By the third inning, she sat wrapped in his arms, feeling passion and the desire to be closer. She shifted, and instead of bumping body parts, their lips met with tenderness. Sometime around the fourth inning, the kisses went from sweet to feverish. Mel shivered.

Clay leaned back. "Cold?"

"Eager, anxious, but not cold." She tugged on his T-shirt. "Impatient and hesitant."

He slid his fingers across her back, trailing kisses down her neck.

She stood, grabbed his right hand, and tugged him toward her bedroom.

Clay stopped. "Are you sure?"

"Are you asking if I think spending the afternoon in your arms is a good idea, or if I want you?"

He grinned before nuzzling her neck with more kisses. "Both."

She tilted her head, moaning when he found the right spot. His words and kisses were honey-sweet and stuck in her thoughts and heart. "Will you settle for one out of two?"

"Sounds like a challenge." His fingertips trailed up and down her spine. "Loser buys dinner." He trailed kisses along her neck.

She pulled him closer as their shadows became one against the bedroom door. *I'm losing this bet.* But she didn't care because she knew she loved and wanted him and not just for today.

****

Outside, the early Sunday evening air still held the heat from the day. After sunset, the air would cool everything but Mel's heart. Memories from this afternoon would keep her warm for the rest of her life. She brushed a hand against Clay's forearm. "Come on, I'll race you two to the car." She giggled, running a tad behind Clay and Kansas.

Clay declared Kansas the winner as he winked at Mel.

Kansas dominated the conversation on the drive to the steak house.

This allowed Mel the opportunity to study Clay. He was a patient driver, never in a rush, and mindful of the other drivers. What she liked best was when their gazes met, and his lazy smile turned wickedly sexy. This afternoon, she had given Clay her heart and had no regrets.

He reached over and brushed his fingers across her hand. "Today, I had the best day ever."

"Me, too." Kansas cheered. "What about you, Auntie?"

"Best day ever."

After parking, the three walked hand in hand across the parking lot. Mel held Kansas' hand in the restaurant as she walked past the white-linen-covered tables, illuminated by gentle, flickering candles. Soft elevator music played in the background, and the savory scent of beef searing on a grill had her mouthwatering. A while had passed since she had eaten anything other than chicken fingers and hot dogs.

"Auntie, this is fancy." Before sitting, Kansas brushed her fingers over the cloth napkin. "They have little tablecloths for the silverware."

Moments later, the waitstaff set a Shirley Temple in front of Kansas. She opened her eyes wider. She removed the tiny umbrella. "I'm saving this forever and ever."

Aww. We're both falling for the same man. The next surprise came when a seared ahi tuna appetizer appeared. Mel looked hesitantly at the thin slices of red tuna accompanied by English cucumbers and a beer-mustard sauce. She swallowed before doing her best to smile encouragingly at Kansas. "Looks delicious."

Clay placed a small piece of fish on a white plate with a cucumber and a little sauce. "Try not to get drunk on the beer sauce." He winked, setting the plate in front of Kansas. He cocked an eyebrow at Mel.

"Sure, I'd love to try it." The first bite surprised her. Instead of tasting fishy, the tuna tasted meaty, buttery-tender, and salty. She cut another piece. "This is good."

After the tuna came a petite filet, well-done, with garlic mashed potatoes, chicken strips with fries, and a ribeye with a salad wedge.

Mel scooped up the potatoes. "My favorite." After tasting all the garlic, she winced at the thought of kissing Clay with breath that could slay a dragon. "After dinner, I'll need some breath mints."

He cut into his rare steak, and a look of joy washed over his features. "Watching baseball all afternoon built up my hunger. The food is delicious. Dining out was a great idea."

Even Kansas smacked her lips as she bit into her crispy breaded chicken slices.

Later, when the waitstaff appeared, Mel extended a hand. "Tonight's on me." She slipped her card into the check-presenter. "After all, you won the wager." Mel drove everyone back to the house so Clay could retrieve his truck. Outside in the driveway, she tried to direct Kansas into the house, but the girl wouldn't budge and remained firmly wedged between them. Mel swallowed the disappointment of being unable to convey how much the entire weekend meant and how she wished he could stay a little longer. After an unsatisfying good-bye, Mel stepped inside with Kansas trailing a step behind.

At eight o'clock, Mel tucked Kansas into bed and danced in the kitchen, humming a love song when she heard the phone buzz. *Clay?* She read the screen. "Opal?" She squeezed the phone. "Opal, is everything good?"

"Yes, I'm fine. I wanted to hear about Kansas and her first overnight. Tell me everything."

Mel wished Kansas could be the one to tell Opal about the party, but with the eight-hour time difference, finding a good time to talk proved hard. Kansas started school before Opal returned to her barracks, and at night, Kansas slept while Opal began her day. Mel recounted the tent, games, and dinner. She left out the part about making out with Clay outside their tent, but something in the tone of her voice must have alluded to their romantic endeavor.

"You sound like you like him," Opal sang. "Will I be getting a new brother-in-law?"

"Seriously. Could I fall in love within a week? We have chemistry and a connection. I can talk to him and not have to censor my thoughts. He makes me want to be a better person, to eat healthier, and to act like an aunt instead of a grandma." She plopped into a chair and let out a sigh. "I've never had such deep feelings about anyone. If I don't try, I'll live my life with what-ifs. If he breaks my heart, well, he better not. But if he does, then I will not regret one minute spent together."

"I can't wait to meet this mystery man." Opal laughed. "It's about time you had a little fun."

When Mel ended the call, she danced to her bedroom and slipped her nightgown over her head. She heard her phone buzz. *Clay.*

"Were you sleeping?"

"No, I just finished talking to my sister. She wanted to hear about the overnight. Thank you again." She chatted until midnight and would have kept talking if Clay hadn't disconnected, wishing her goodnight. Would they have chatted until sunrise? Mel hugged her pillow. She tried to close her eyelids, but the day's events left her wide-eyed and unable to sleep. She recalled all the tender, sweet moments and wondered if she should let Paula know she had been right about a happy-ever-after ending for her and Clay.

****

On Monday morning, Mel opened her eyes to Kansas dancing around her bedroom.

"Wake up, sleepy Auntie," she sang. "It's my last week of school."

Mel stretched. "I don't suppose you made me coffee?"

"Auntie, go get dressed. If you hurry, we might have time to go to the coffee shop. And if you behave, you can have whipped cream."

She laughed. "You sound like me. What have you done with my niece?"

"Hurry, hurry, hurry." She pushed her toward the closet. "Get your clothes on. I'll pack a snack and get my backpack." Kansas led the morning preparation.

Mel slipped into the car with plenty of time to drive by the coffee shop. She sat across from Kansas at an outdoor table, eating an egg bite, and sipping coffee. "What's your favorite thing about summer?" Mel asked.

"That's easy. No homework, and my mom comes home."

"A couple more months." Mel leaned across the table and brushed a stray curl from Kansas' eyes. "She'll be so happy to see you. I know she misses you a lot."

As soon as she uttered the words, she remembered her forgotten promise to send Opal the photos and made a mental note to send them. With the sun warming her shoulders as she listened to Kansas chatting, she smiled. *What a perfect morning!*

After the day care drop-off, she drove to Gascon with her windows open. She ambled through the lot, inhaling the sweet smell of lilacs and stopping at the

Construction Dunn Wright truck. She reached into her backpack, grabbed a sticky note, drew a big smiley face with lots of added hearts, and stuck her artwork on Clay's side mirror.

As she imagined his reaction to the artwork, she grinned. The giddy feeling stayed as she took the stairs to the basement and stepped into her office. She blinked. A new desk accessory. *Flowers.* She rushed to the enormous bouquet of roses and baby's breath. "Aw," slipped between her parted lips as the familiar sound of *tap-tap-tap* echoed across her office floor. "Hello, Paula."

"Oh, look. Look." She tapped her steps in an overtime tempo. "Roses. Red." Paula stopped and narrowed her gaze. "You know, they say a man always sends flowers after…"

Mel fanned her cheeks with both hands and swallowed.

"Yes." Paula danced to the exit. "I predicted the happily-ever-after ending."

She tugged her clinging shirt from her stomach and stooped to smell the flowers. *The baby's breath smells sweet, but not as sweet as Clay.* She shook her head. *When did I become so sappy?*

—*Hey, handsome. Thanks for the flowers. I love them.*—

—*My pleasure. This entire weekend has been my pleasure. I only hope you feel the same way.*—

Mel sent a sweet reply and set her phone aside. She turned on her computer, but an hour later, she sent him another text. The dance of work and having a social life continued until five o'clock when she switched her computer off and met Paula at the elevator. "Want to take the stairs today?"

Paula raised an eyebrow. "Sure thing."

On the way to the first floor, Mel talked about her plans for dinner at Clay's house.

"Do you need me to watch Kansas?"

"Not tonight. I'm only stopping by for dinner."

Paula winked. "Sure, you are."

"But I'll take a raincheck on the offer for babysitting. Maybe I'll ask Clay on a date?"

****

After getting home from day care, Mel barely had time to change and spritz on a bit of perfume. *Will Kansas be on her best behavior or her worst?* She grabbed the deodorant and added another layer of protection. If everything went well, they could all do backyard cookouts or holiday dinners when Opal returned. *We haven't gone on a date, and I'm making long-term plans. Paula has rubbed off on me.*

One more week of school and Mel could relax the evening routine of homework, bath, and bedtime story, but they still had a schedule to keep tonight. "Come on, Kansas." Mel reached for the remote, took a deep breath, and shut off the television.

Kansas hopped off the sofa. "Come on, Auntie. I'm ready, too."

A long breath whistled between her lips. *I'm not the only one excited to see Clay.* They arrived at his house at six. Mel opened her eyes wider as they stepped into the house. His choice of a blue-collar café did not match the artful decor in the vaulted spaces of his home. "Nice open floor plan." She glanced at a framed painting. "Village in South America?" She stepped closer to study the colors.

"Yes, a Chilean artist painted it. I forget the town's name, but I like the bright colors and contrast."

"It brightens the room. Your house is so not a bachelor pad. I don't know what I expected, but this is nice and tasteful."

He lifted a single eyebrow. "Yes, no sawhorses or motorcycles in the living room. Or maybe you thought I'd have a beer can collection on the wall."

"Work has been my life; besides my sister, I only talk to Paula. I guess I didn't realize the world had evolved since college. If my comments offend you, I apologize. I thought your house would look more like mine. Plain, stark, and mismatched, but your home is gorgeous."

"Thank you again. I enjoy coming home, and I enjoy cooking. I have an apron for anyone who wants to help me with dinner." He winked and flashed a quick, quirky smile.

"I do, I do." Kansas jumped up and down. "I do, I do."

He handed the apron to Kansas. "Make yourself at home. We'll be in the kitchen if you need us."

"Uncle, you have a smiling face with hearts on your fridge. Who gave you the picture?"

Mel froze. *Will Kansas have a meltdown if she knows I am dating Clay? Will she feel like we're vying for the same man?*

"Do you want to color me a picture after dinner?" She heard Clay ask. "I can put your artwork on the refrigerator, too."

Nice deflection. He avoided answering the question and made her feel special. After making a mental note to implement the same strategy the next time Kansas

84

became difficult, she walked down the hall to the dining room. The glow of the setting sun bathed the dark oak table and illuminated a series of photographs on the wall. She moved closer to the photo of a younger Clay posed with a distinguished gentleman before a plate-glass window with *ABC Accounting* etched across the glass. She tapped her bottom lip with a finger. Why had he hung this photo? Did he regret the falling out with his father?

The evening flew by, and before Mel wanted to say good-bye, they stood beside the car as Kansas climbed into the backseat and buckled her car seat. Mel shut the door and stepped out of her niece's vision, before wrapping her arms around Clay.

His arms tightened around her.

Mel leaned back. "She should be asleep by nine."

"And?" He smiled.

"I won't be." She winked.

He leaned close but didn't kiss her. He lowered his hands to her hips and brushed his lips against her ear. "See you at nine."

She kissed his cheek. "I'll be waiting."

****

On Tuesday morning, Clay slipped out the door before Kansas woke up.

They both agreed they didn't want Kansas to be aware of his overnights. After kissing him good-bye, she searched her closet, donned a pair of clean pants, and rushed to make coffee. She scowled at the last of her coffee grounds and adjusted the waist of her pants. *I'll catch up on my emails, laundry, and grocery shopping tonight.* Mel grabbed the steamy coffee, raised her cup, and vowed to get it together. *A fresh start for me and a successful last week for Kansas.* As she waited for Kansas to finish getting ready in the bathroom, she sipped her coffee and composed an email.

Opal, I'm a little late in sending the photos. To be honest, I am not sure how single parents manage their kids' calendars, work, and social lives. The pictures are from the sleepover and a couple of selfies we took at Clay's house last night. Besides having you as a sister and Kansas as a niece, he is the best thing that has happened to me. You'll like him.

She attached the photos to the email and hit Send.

Kansas bounced into the kitchen, singing about the last week of school and the need to hurry.

Mel took the hint and raced her to the car.

Later at work, Paula tap-danced into her office. "Hey, Boss Lady, I heard a rumor about moving to the fourth floor on Monday and nonsense about overtime this summer. Any truth?"

Mel pushed back from her desk. "Pack up your desk before you leave work on Friday, and come Monday, you can unpack upstairs. As far as overtime goes, I'm behind on email correspondence. Hopefully, I'll get through my emails and let you know."

"Boss Lady." Paula cleared her throat and stepped closer. "I know covering for Bill put you behind, but—" She tugged the beaded fringe on her pleather skirt.

"You heard people complaining. I know. Sometimes, I think I should have turned down the promotion last year. Maybe I'm not cut out for the job."

Paula shrugged. "You're more like a friend than a boss."

"I'm too nice. I know. Order lunch for the team

and get me something good with a diet soda." Mel shifted her gaze back to her computer.

"Yep, that's why you're the best." Paula tapped her toes.

Mel sighed. *Why do I always have to choose? Friend or boss? Aunt or caregiver?*

****

On Tuesday night, instead of going to the park, Mel let Kansas play games on an electronic device and went into her office. She refocused her thoughts as her mind wandered from her business communications to Clay. She could still feel his touch on her skin and the taste of his lips. Sighing, she caught sight of the time on the bottom of her screen. *Oh, no. Nine o'clock.* "Kansas, all done. Time for bed, honey."

Kansas stared at the tablet. "I'm not tired."

Now, how had Clay done the deflection? "Okay, I'll be in your bedroom, reading one of your favorite stories to your stuffed animals."

She scrambled from the sofa. "Wait. I want to hear the stories, too."

"Okay, hurry then." After reading *Living Things,* she rubbed Kansas' back for fifteen minutes. "Close your eyes. Shh," Mel repeated until her niece's breath became soft and steady. She tiptoed back to her office and spotted an email from Opal on her personal account. She read the subject line.

For Your Eyes Only

Did they extend Opal's deployment? She gripped the desk's edge. The pounding of her heart echoed in her ears. When the room spun, she reached back for her chair and collapsed. *How will I break the news to Kansas?* She took a ragged breath and, with shaking fingers, maneuvered the mouse to open the letter.

"No!" She covered her mouth with her left hand and read through her tears. The knots in her stomach twisted, and she swallowed. Reading hurt, but she needed to finish. Every word tore at her heart. She clutched her chest, wondering if she'd ever feel anything but pain and dread.

AFTER READING, DELETE THIS EMAIL.

Tears streamed down her cheeks as she followed Opal's instructions. She shuddered and tried to swallow down the pain. After ten minutes, she took a large breath but couldn't move from the chair. *Never see Clay.* On leaden legs, she stood and staggered down the hall, into the bedroom, and collapsed on the mattress. *How can I fix this? Think.*

Chapter Nine

Thirty minutes after reading Opal's letter, Mel flipped over the tear-soaked pillow and climbed from the bed. She tugged off her crumpled clothes and slipped a nightshirt over her head. Kansas still had three days of school. *What should I do?*

She crawled back into bed and focused on counting backward from a thousand. One thousand, nine hundred and ninety-nine. Clay's firm but gentle lips. Nine hundred and ninety-eight. He had my yard mowed. Nine hundred and ninety-seven. He put up a tent and organized games for Kansas' friends. Nine hundred and ninety-six. My head on his chest, and the warmth of his smile...

Mel woke up with a start. She checked the time: two hours before daylight. She closed her eyes and wished she never had to open them again. Feelings of sorrow and despair gave way to hope. *I'll call Opal. I'll reason with her.* She hopped out of bed and shut the door. She paced around her room, waiting for Opal to answer.

"Opal, I've given this a lot of thought. I'll be careful. You don't have to worry. I know Clay. He won't do anything rash or stupid." Mel sniffled as her happiness changed to despair. "Opal, be reasonable. I know you're upset. Opal, please calm down." She nodded and paced for three more minutes. "Yes, yes.

Stop crying. I'll swear, Opal, on your life and Kansas' life, I won't see him, I promise." She disconnected, crawled into bed, and cried for another hour. She pulled at her raw throat, swiped her puffy eyes, and stumbled to the bathroom. The hot shower spray mixed with her salty tears, but it did nothing to stop the ache in her body. After she toweled herself dry, she did her best to make herself presentable with concealer and red-reducing eye drops. She forced her cheeks into a smile and walked into Kansas' room. "Wake up, sleepyhead."

Kansas scrambled out of bed and rubbed her eyes. "Auntie, you don't look so good. What's wrong?"

"I must have caught a cold or something. But I'll be fine. Come on. We need to get you to day care."

At work, she walked through the front door with dark sunglasses and greeted no one before shutting herself into her office. She stumbled to the desk, collapsed into her chair, and texted Paula.

—*Don't call unless the building is burning. I don't want to talk to anyone, not even you.*—

At her desk, Mel struggled to keep her eyes focused through the tears while sinking into a sea of uncertainty and despair. Mel didn't want to cause Opal further pain or have Kansas caught in a custody battle. According to the US Army Family Plan, Mel was Kansas' closest blood relative and had sole responsibility for Kansas, so she had to grant Opal her request.

She closed her eyes. *When Opal returns, I'll tell Clay everything, but will he wait?* She opened her eyes and stared at the unanswered emails. She blinked back more tears. *Why did I even bother coming to work today?*

Hearing her phone buzz lifted her spirits. Had Opal reconsidered? She shook her heavy head. *Clay.* She slumped farther into her chair.

—Mel, what's going on? Paula's a bulldog and won't let me see you or tell me why.—

After reading the fifth text he sent, she switched the phone to silent and rubbed her temples. How can I continue a relationship with Clay, knowing what I know? Opal will hate me, and I'll never see Kansas again. She closed her eyes, suppressing memories of his passionate kisses and the heat from his touch. Slowly, she opened her eyes, hoping to find strength in memories with her family. *Opal constantly makes sacrifices, even risking her life to serve our country.* Mel leaned over until her forehead rested on her folded arms. *Nothing changes; I spent my life protecting Opal and wanting to keep her safe, but I also want to love Clay. Why am I still not grateful for what I have?*

At four o'clock, she shut off her computer, slipped on her dark sunglasses, and told Paula she could find her at home if she needed anything. She gazed at her feet as she walked out of the office and through the parking lot to her car.

"Mel."

At the sound of his voice, she tilted her head, her pulse quickened, and she had to stop herself from rushing to him. "Clay. What are you doing here?"

"Waiting for you."

She drew in three ragged breaths before her lungs inflated. She focused on her license plate. "There is something…" The words came out in puffs as she struggled to suck in enough air. "If there was any other way." Sweat beaded on her upper lip. "There isn't, and

I can't see you anymore."

"What? Why?" He rushed forward.

She flashed her palms up, as if she were stopping a speeding car from crashing into her. "Don't come any closer." His scent of woods, beach, and summer drifted past. She lowered her gaze and shifted.

"Why, Mel?"

"The photo of you and your dad." Her words rushed from her mouth. "You're standing in front of his accounting firm." She took another deep breath and glanced in his direction.

His gaze penetrated her sunglasses as he shifted closer.

She dropped her focus to the keys, jingling in her sweaty hands.

"I told you I worked for my dad."

"Yeah, well." She rocked onto her toes, glancing at the cars beside her. "You also said you quit." She shifted from side to side. "You didn't work things out with him or even go after Liz. I don't want to waste my time." She swallowed the lump in her throat. "I need someone strong and willing to fight for what they want. Not someone who will disappear at the first sign of trouble." She unlocked the door with her fob.

Clay brushed her hand aside and opened her door.

Why? Why is he understanding? He should rant, deny, or race back to his truck. Why can't he leave? The car door opened, and she fell into the driver's seat. The door-ajar alarm buzzed. She clenched the steering wheel and dropped her forehead onto her clamped fingers. The door alarm stopped. She glanced out the side window.

He stood beside the closed door, his bottom lip

trembling as he gave a slight wave.

After three attempts, she swallowed down the lump of hot, burning agony. The fire seared a path to the pit of her stomach. When the pain subsided, she searched the lot but didn't see Clay. She sighed, knowing she still had to drive to Kansas' school and face the lineup of moms picking up kids. How did Opal become so strong? *This situation is nothing compared to what Opal faces every day.* Mel found new courage in her shame. She imagined Opal sitting next to her. "Dry those tears up, soldier. We still have work to do."

Mel rushed Kansas into the car and drove home without letting her hear the pain in her voice or see the cracks in her armor. But how long could she pull off pretending to be brave?

****

On Thursday morning, Mel awoke to Kansas singing.

"Open your eyes, sleepyhead. Auntie, wake up."

"One more minute."

"No." Kansas stomped her feet. "Hurry, hurry, hurry."

"Fine. Go get your backpack." Mel tossed on the first thing her fingers touched, brushed her hair, and dabbed concealer beneath her eyes. She glared at her reflection.

Kansas rushed into the bathroom. "Auntie, hurry."

Mel tried to hustle, but her legs moved like she wore cement slippers. She hated herself for checking every few minutes to see if Clay had sent a message. *I'm glad he hasn't texted.* She repeated the sour confession every time she glanced at the phone. After grabbing her bag, she stumbled to the front door.

Kansas pushed her from behind. "Come on, Auntie."

Somehow, Mel got Kansas to day care and drove to work without mishaps. She held her head high and marched into the building, vowing to keep her personal life out of the office. At the end of the workday, she exhaled: no sightings of Clay, and Paula hadn't danced into her office.

However, Kansas presented a forgotten dilemma on Thursday night. At the kitchen table, Kansas dragged a fast-food fry through her ketchup. "Where's my uncle?"

Mel shrugged and bit into a fried fish sandwich. White, creamy tartar sauce dripped down her chin.

"Auntie, in my backpack, I have more pictures for Uncle. I want to see him. Come on. Call him."

"Maybe, later. I have work to finish. Why don't you color some more?"

Kansas jumped from her chair and stomped her feet. "No, no, no. I want my uncle."

What did Clay do to get Kansas back on board? *Diversion, distraction, persuasion, or something? Persuasive, warm kisses and strong hands stroking my hair...*

"Hello." Kansas turned up the volume. "Can you hear me? Call my uncle."

"Honey. Clay's working a lot." Mel hated lying, but she couldn't think of another option. "Let's hop in the car and see if we can find him at his favorite restaurant."

Kansas nodded. "We could save this food for tomorrow."

Mel shoved the remaining meals back into the

paper sack.

After getting into the car, she drove to a family fast-food restaurant and hoped to distract Kansas with an oversized play area, multiple slides, and a colorful ball pit. But Kansas refused to eat or join the other kids.

She sat in the plastic booth with tightly folded arms. "Auntie, he isn't here. Where else can we look?"

"Sometimes, he goes shopping at the superstore." Mel stood, stuffed their untouched oversized drinks into the trash, and drove the two miles to the store. "Let's see if we can find him." She rubbed her pounding temples hoping to ease the tension before grabbing a cart.

"Auntie—"

"Look at those sandals." Mel pointed, not wanting to hear another question about Clay. "Super cute. Why don't you try them on?" In the toy aisle, she bought a few more minutes of peace and quiet. Around nine o'clock, she drove home. The evening sky had darkened, and Mel yawned when she followed Kansas through the front door of the house. Tonight, she didn't bother to check Kansas' backpack for homework or start a bath. When seeing Kansas happily crawl into bed with her brand-new Fritz, the friendly fire dog, and a sleepy-eye doll, Mel sighed.

At a little after ten, Mel remembered to plug in her phone. She opened her eyes wider and shook her head. *Ten text messages and a voicemail…all from Clay. Is he fighting for me? Or is he dumping me?* She ignored the texts and played back the recorded voice message.

"Mel, I have a few things I want to tell you. Please call. Love you."

Clay loves me. She welcomed the fluttering

sensation in her stomach and sank into the bed. A shot of adrenaline mixed with fear bolted her upright and tensed her muscles. Maybe he called to say good-bye because he has an out-of-state or out-of-country job. *What if this is my last opportunity to hear his voice? I won't break my promise to Opal if I only listen.*

With the phone pressed tight against her ear, she counted the rings. She glanced at the clock. *After eleven. Should I hang up?*

"Hello."

The sound of his voice chased away her fatigue, and she smiled. "I'm so sorry. I didn't see you had called. Kansas wanted to go to the store. We completely—"

"It's okay. I just called to say *thanks*. After some soul-searching, I called my dad. It turns out I wasn't as bright as I imagined back then. The photo hanging in my dining room reminds me that family is important. I also called Liz. I won't repeat what she said before hanging up. In hindsight, I should have told Liz I didn't want to get married."

She sniffed, brushed a tear from her cheek, and hugged her pillow. He had confronted his past for her. *He's doing everything right and doesn't even know the truth. Should I tell him and break my promise to Opal? What do I do?* She set the pillow down.

"Mel, say something? Anything? Just let me know you're still there."

She cleared her throat.

"Is everything okay?"

"I'm fine. Kansas is fine. Opal is fine."

"Opal?"

"My sister, Opal, doesn't—" She pursed her lips

tight and held her breath.

"Your sister's name is Opal?"

The surprise and suspicion in his voice had Mel clutching her stomach and swallowing the sour taste of bile. She couldn't believe she hadn't mentioned her sister's name before. Had she said too much?

"I dated an Opal. Is your sister an occupational therapist?"

Mel exhaled and drew in another breath as the pounding of her heart beat against her chest. "I hear Kansas. I'll talk to you later." She disconnected. Had she just done what Opal instructed her not to do? She heard the phone buzz with a text.

—*Mel, did you send Opal a selfie of us?*—

A second text.

—*Why would Opal care? I haven't seen her in six or seven years. I had broken up with Liz. Opal was in Kansas for work.*—

She tucked the buzzing phone under her pillow. *Think, think, think.* She slipped the silent phone out. He had sent another text.

—*Is Kansas my daughter?*—

Her pact with her sister unraveled before her eyes. She swallowed down the bitter taste in the back of her throat. *How could I be so stupid?* Opal isn't a common first name. Of course, Clay would put two and two together. Mel swallowed again and clenched her hands to stop them from shaking. Should she hire a lawyer? Or ask Clay. But what? Not to see his daughter? Not to acknowledge Kansas' existence? Before she could think straight, she heard her phone buzz with another text.

—*Mel, how long have you known?*—

She typed half a dozen responses and deleted each

before hitting Send. Clay deserved an answer, but if Opal's right, he'll take Kansas. She shook her head. *Opal doesn't know him the way I do. Clay won't be rash.*

   —*Mel, talk to me.*—
   —*Please!*—
Buzz, buzz, buzz.

A sinking sensation in her gut caused her to glare at the ringing phone. *What if I'm wrong? Can he take Kansas? Will he want Opal back? Are these the reasons I didn't tell him he's a father?* "Stop, stop, I need time to think," she muttered. "Please, stop." She shut her eyes tight and then opened them. *If I don't answer, will he rush over and bang on the door? Will Kansas wake up?* After the fourth ring, she knew he wasn't giving up. "Hello."

"Talk to me, Mel. How long have you known? Does Kansas know? Why didn't Opal contact me? I would have helped her. My daughter should know her dad. I've missed out on so much. My God, she's already six years old. I don't even know her birthday. Mel, say something."

She rested a hand on her pounding heart and drew in a breath. "Opal is six thousand miles away, and we're both worried you'll want custody of Kansas. She didn't abandon Kansas to go on a vacation. She's a soldier, deployed to Kuwait, serving our country."

"When will she be back?"

"August. She comes home in August, so if you can wait. I don't want to fight you, but I will—"

"Mel, I have no idea what you're thinking. Or why?"

"Clay." She pressed the phone tight against her ear.

"Clay?" *How could he hang up?* She glared at the screen and resisted throwing the phone across the room. *What would Clay do now? Would he get a lawyer? Do I need a lawyer?* She curled into a fetal position, clutching the phone. *If he loved me, he'd trust me to do what's best. How do I tell Opal I screwed up?* Mel sighed, buried the phone under her pillow, and yanked the covers over her head. She could feel slow, wet tears slide across her cheek and plop onto her pillow. Too exhausted to wipe them away, she let them fall as she fell into a restless sleep.

Opal stood in her uniform beside a towering pine tree in a heavily wooded forest. She shouted, "Kansas, Kansas, where are you?"

Mel flapped her arms, waved, and pointed, hoping Opal would look up. Kansas was near the top of the tree, but Opal only focused on the ground.

"Uncle, where are you?" Kansas shouted.

"Opal, look up, look up!" Mel pointed.

The tree trunk Clay was climbing split up the middle. He straddled both halves as he shouted, "Mel, make a soft landing for Kansas. I'll hang on as long as you need me to. I won't let go."

Mel tore branches from the bush and threw them in a pile.

"Here she comes," Clay hollered.

She glanced at her armload of grasses and leaves. "No, wait. I'm not ready."

"Auntie, catch me. Auntie."

Mel opened her eyes.

"Auntie, Auntie." Kansas stood next to the bed. "You threw a pillow at me. I'm here to sing you awake, and you tossed your pillow. You're silly in the mornings." Kansas brushed the hair from Mel's eyes. "Are you awake?"

"Are you hurt?" Mel tried to recall the distancing fragments of her dream.

"No. Hurry. Or we'll be late for my last day of school."

"Go make your bed, and I'll start breakfast." Mel waved her right arm toward the door and picked up her phone. No messages. She swallowed down the pain and blinked to keep away the tears. Mel sighed. *Should I have trusted Clay with the truth? Does he hate me? What do I do?*

Chapter Ten

On Friday morning, Mel stepped outside the house. The sky rumbled with black clouds, and the air smelled like rain.

Kansas danced to the car, singing, "Last day of school."

"Yep, Friday. No more school after today." She checked her phone. *Why hasn't he texted?* She swallowed. *Is it over between us? Am I being unreasonable?* She clenched her hands. *Of course, finding out he's a dad is confusing, and the news shocked me, too.* Still, if he was who she thought he was, he'd understand the difficult position of having a sister deployed. With effort, she forced herself to smile. *I will not make Kansas pay the price for having unreasonable parents.* "Hey, kiddo, what did you like best about first grade?"

She climbed silently into the backseat; she drummed a finger on her bottom lip. Ten minutes later, she filled the car with chatter and rattled off numerous likes, everything from clothes, lunches, boys, girls, and teachers.

Mel pulled into a vacant spot in the child care parking lot and took three deep breaths. *You got this. Suit of armor, suit of armor, suit of armor, go.* She pressed the release button three times on her seat belt before the lock disengaged. The back door slammed.

"Kansas. Stop!" She jumped from the driver's seat.

With her arms pumping, Kansas dashed behind a small sports car.

"Kansas, you need to hold my hand." Mel caught hold of her shoulder before she stepped behind a van.

"Sorry, I forgot."

Fear clenched her jaw, and Mel swallowed words of reprimand for not following the rules. She blinked back tears, feeling powerless in her ability to keep Kansas safe. "It's hard for the cars to see you. If something happened to you." With trembling arms and a racing heart, she gathered Kansas close.

"I know, Auntie." Kansas nodded as they held hands and walked into the day care center. "Today, we have our assembly program. There will be ribbons and awards. Alyssa told me the best ones are blue."

She nodded and stooped to say good-bye. "Have a good day."

"Auntie!"

"Yeah. What, honey?" Mel brushed crumbs from her niece's shirt.

"I said," Kansas placed her hands on Mel's cheeks. "I hope you and Uncle come to the program. The note is in my backpack."

She bit her lip and swallowed down the words. *Why didn't you tell me?*

Kansas plopped the backpack on the ground and worked to get the zipper open. Crammed inside were dozens of papers, books, and artwork, but somehow, she pulled out a single sheet. "Will you and Uncle come?" She danced. "Please, Auntie, please, please."

"Of course, I'll come and invite Clay."

The invitation in her hands shook on the way to the

car. *I almost missed her program. I can't change the past, but I'm not screwing up Kansas' future.*

****

She didn't remember walking into work; yet, she stood before her desk. *Pull yourself together. You're a manager and a caregiver. You've done harder stuff. Remember, work and home life don't mix. Be a professional.*

"Boss Lady," Paula called from the doorway. "I brought you some coffee. Safe to come in?"

Mel walked around her desk and sat. "Yes."

"You walked past me without even saying hello." Paula walked over and set the cup on the desk. Is everything okay with your family?"

"Opal and Kansas are good." Her voice cracked.

"That leaves Clayton."

Mel rubbed a hand across her chest and nodded.

"Want to talk about it?"

"No." The word rushed from her mouth. She didn't even want to think about the situation. Yet she couldn't shift her thoughts from thinking about what she should have said or done.

Paula strode to the doorway and hesitated. "If you need anything at all, let me know."

"Thanks." Mel pulled out her phone. *No new messages.* She closed her eyes. *Am I right in believing Clay will do what's best for Kansas? Or is Opal correct in assuming he'll fight for custody before she returns?* She took a deep breath. *Think.* She tried to imagine Opal's disappointment and frustration at being thousands of miles away and being blindsided by something she hadn't planned.

She swallowed down the sour taste rising from her

stomach. *I'm the big sister and should take care of Opal, not rip her heart in two by telling her I let Clay know he's a dad.* But before apologizing to Opal, she had to be a traitor one last time. She typed the message to Clay as her insides squeezed her heart and stomach.

—*Kansas has a school program at one o'clock today. I just found out this morning. Kansas wanted me to invite her Uncle Clayton. Will you please come?*—

She gulped the coffee and cringed as her stomach cramped. *When did I last eat?* She could feel her stomach lurch and gurgle before tightening. The room tilted, and she placed one hand firmly on the desk. *I should have eaten breakfast.* Setting her phone down, she stood on wobbling legs. *Why didn't I grab a banana or snack pack?* She paused in the doorway. Paula always hides snacks in her desk.

At the sight of Paula's empty desk drawer, she sighed and took the elevator to the third floor. Halfway down the hall, she sucked in air to dislodge the feeling of heaviness. She turned the corner, the lights flickered, and a powerful arm wrapped around her waist. She blinked and sniffed the subtle scent of cedar and citrus. "Clay?"

"Are you okay?" He cupped her elbow with his free hand. "You're as white as a sheet."

"I missed breakfast. Just a little light-headed. I'll be fine."

"Let me help you to the lunchroom." Inside, he motioned to an empty table and pulled out a chair. "Sit."

She collapsed into the blue-molded plastic and watched him return with a water bottle and a granola bar. She tried to smile. "Thanks."

He screwed the top off the bottle, unwrapped the bar, and set them next to Mel.

"The program," she said, in between sips of water. "At Kansas' school at one. There will be awards. I sent you a text."

"Got it and I—"

"Mel," Paula shouted.

"I'm in the lunchroom." A shiver ran down her spine. "Something's wrong."

"Mel, Mel." Paula skidded across the tile floors. "You left your cell phone in the office. The school nurse called. Kansas fell at recess. The school nurse—"

"What?" Mel sprung from her chair, clutching her chest. "Did they take Kansas to the hospital?" She grasped the edge of the table, feeling hot and clammy as a knot tightened in her stomach.

Paula shook her head. "No, Kansas has a little swelling in her wrist and is at the school office. But otherwise, she's fine."

The room spun as the pounding of her heart echoed in her ears. She grabbed for the table. Strong hands clasped her shoulders.

"Sit."

Mel shook free of his grasp. "Kansas needs me."

"You don't look like you should be driving. I'll take you." Concern etched deep lines around his eyes. His gaze darkened, and he gave a slight shake of his head.

"Okay, but I need my bag and my phone."

Paula held up both. "Let me know how she is."

"Yes. Yes." Mel struggled to inflate her lungs as she increased her pace.

Clay never let go of her right arm as they hustled to

his truck. "She'll be okay." He opened the passenger door.

"Wait." Mel shook her car keys. "She still needs a booster seat. We need to take my car." Mel drained the water bottle as they walked. Inside the car, she shouted instructions. "A left on Third Street and take the entrance ramp to the freeway. Hurry."

At the school, with Clay by her side, she rushed to the security guard, who gave directions to the front office.

A nurse removed the ice pack from Kansas' wrist. "You have a brave little girl."

"Uncle," Kansas squealed. "Are you here for my program? I might get a ribbon."

He leaned down. "I'm happy to see you, too. How's your wrist?"

She waved her arms. "I was running fast, faster than Alyssa. My sandals flew off, and splat, I hit the ground. See." She held up her palm and pointed to the scrape on her right knee. "It hurt at first, but I didn't even cry. They made me see the nurse, anyway."

Mel signed her niece out and thanked the nurse before motioning for Kansas to follow. "Come on, honey, Uncle will drive us to urgent care." On the drive to the clinic, Mel kept turning to check on Kansas, even though she hadn't stopped talking since Clay buckled her booster seat. Before exiting the car, Mel reminded Kansas she had to hold someone's hand in the busy parking lot.

The late morning sun glared off the windows of the eight-story yellow brick-and-glass medical center. Mel squinted as she followed Clay and Kansas across the massive tar parking lot. Before stepping inside, Mel pressed her hand across her chest, hoping to slow the pounding, but the tempo only increased.

Inside, Clay pointed the way toward the urgent care clinic.

"It smells funny." Kansas wrinkled her nose. "Can we go?"

Mel didn't hear Clay's response to Kansas as she imagined the worst. *What if Kansas needs surgery?* The more she thought, the faster her heart beat. Standing beside the receptionist's desk, Mel clutched the edge of the desk as the room spun. "I have her medical card in my purse." After letting go of the desk, she swayed, bumping against Clay.

The receptionist pointed. "Does she need a wheelchair?"

"No. What? I'm fine." Mel waved Kansas' medical card. "My heart—I can hear my heartbeats echoing in my ears."

A nurse rushed forward and placed an arm around Mel. "Come with me."

Did the receptionist hit a panic button? "No. I need to stay. My niece is hurt. I'm fine."

Clay brushed Mel's forearm. "Don't worry. I'll stay with Kansas."

Mel didn't have the energy to struggle with the nurse as she ushered her through the door and down the hall to an exam room. An hour later, she rushed back into the waiting room and smiled.

Huddled together in the children's play area, Clay and Kansas sat reading the same book.

Clay jumped up. "Are you okay? What did the doctor say? You had us worried." He wrapped an arm around her waist.

"Dehydration and stress." She leaned in closer. "Is her arm broken?"

"She has a sprained wrist and wears the splint for two weeks. I scheduled the re-check appointment. We need to ice it, keep her wrist elevated, and no running with sandals for a while—"

"Hurry." Kansas waved her splint. "My program is this afternoon."

Thirty minutes later, Mel and Clay escorted Kansas to the office.

The receptionist let everyone know the program would start in fifteen minutes, and she'd escort Kansas back to class.

After saying good-bye, Mel could feel Clay's hand on her elbow as she followed the signs to the auditorium. The student's artwork lining the hall walls blurred... *How do I tell Opal? Who will tell Kansas?* Mel rubbed her sternum and took a deep breath.

Clay's grip tightened. "Are you okay?"

"Never better." She dropped her hand and forced a smile. "Come on, let's go find a seat."

He wanted to sit right in front so Kansas couldn't miss him, but they settled for the center of the second row.

Mel leaned back. In a couple of months, Opal would be home. *Would she forgive me?* She took a slow, deep breath. *I should let Clay know I'm sorry. He's a good man. I should have told Opal she didn't have to worry about him doing the wrong thing.*

A warm hand rested on her knee. "Remember when I asked you if you trusted me?"

His words brushed softly against her ear. Mel held her breath. *Is this a question or a statement?*

"Do you still trust me?"

She rested a hand on his knee and gazed deep into his eyes. "I do trust you." She drew a big breath, and as she exhaled, the tension in her shoulders eased. "I'm sorry. I let fear get the better of me."

"It's okay. Sometimes, we all do crazy things when we are scared." He smiled.

All the worrying had been wasted time. *Clay's a good guy.* She sighed and relaxed her shoulders. "I'm sorry. I didn't tell you any sooner."

He wound his fingers through hers. "We'll figure this out together."

A woman plopped down beside Clay. "What grade is your child in?"

Mel leaned over Clay. "His daughter is in first grade." As she settled back into her seat, she watched Clay turn. His left eyebrow arched slightly, and his gaze softened, conveying more love than she had imagined possible.

The lights in the audience dimmed, and the program began with a line of anxious students lined up from the exit doors to the side stage steps.

Kansas appeared on stage, and he released Mel's hand and shifted his attention to capturing the moment on his phone.

She raced to the center of the stage, gripping her certificate for completing first grade. She peered into the rows of seats. "Uncle, Auntie," Kansas shouted and waved. "I have a certificate."

Everyone clapped, and Kansas accepted a blue ribbon for being the most helpful.

Mel debated whether Kansas or Clay had the biggest smile. A tear ran down the side of her nose.

This time, no sting accompanied it, and she welcomed another.

After the program concluded, Kansas rode in the car instead of taking the bus to the after-school program.

As they drove, Mel texted Paula to let her know she'd be taking the rest of the day off, and Kansas had sprained her wrist.

Unfortunately, Clay had to work. They had a final inspection on Monday, and he needed to check his crew's progress.

"Uncle." Kansas waved her ribbon from the backseat. "Can you come over tonight?"

He parked next to his work truck but didn't respond.

Mel suspected he wanted her to decide. "We love having you over, but not tonight. I need to send Opal an email." She mouthed, *sorry*. Then she puckered her lips and blew him a kiss.

"You're so mean, Auntie. We never get to have any fun."

"Kansas." Clay turned toward the backseat. "I don't like to hear words that make Auntie feel sad. Can you think of any words that would make her happy?"

Mel swallowed down words of protest. She wanted to tell Clay that Kansas didn't mean it. To stop herself from saying the words, she chewed on her bottom lip as she exited the car and walked around to the driver's side.

Clay stood outside the open backseat car door. "Kansas, do you have anything to say?"

"Auntie, Uncle, thank you for coming to my program."

"Great job, kiddo." He ducked his head inside and brushed a hand across the top of her curls. "And you should be so proud of yourself for getting a blue ribbon for being the biggest helper. I need a helper."

"Me!" Kansas squealed. "I can be your helper."

He straightened and tapped an index finger to his chin. "You might be too little. My helper needs to water each plant."

Still buckled into her booster seat, Kansas flayed her arms. "I'm strong. I can drag the hose across the yard."

"Even with one arm?"

Kansas examined her splint. "Yes, I can water with one arm."

Clay rested a hand on Mel's forearm. "Will you be okay?"

"The doctor suggested the typical. Drink water, rest, blah, blah, blah. My heart's well."

He clasped her hand. "The incident with your heart gave me quite the scare."

She searched his eyes for all the love she had seen earlier. And once again, passion, love, and desire beckoned her to him. She quieted the noise in her head. *For now, I will enjoy every moment with him, and later, I'll tell him about my need to follow up with a cardiologist.*

"Would you be okay with me checking on you and Kansas?"

Mel let go of his hand and leaned into him.

He wrapped an arm around her.

The strength of his embrace brought her into contact with the heat from his body. Instead of sweet cedar, she caught the scent of fear and a long day.

"Sure, but not tonight. I have something I have to do first."

"Of course, but promise to call me if you need anything."

Did her word mean anything anymore? She had failed to keep her promise to Opal. Would she break more promises? She hugged him tighter. "I will."

Chapter Eleven

Friday night, after a dozen failed attempts at composing an apology to Opal, Mel walked out of her office and lay down on her bed. *If only Opal instantly grants me forgiveness or trusts me to make the right decisions.* She shook her head. *All my life, I've made everyone's life easier. Harold tried to tell me I didn't have to take responsibility for the way people reacted to the news. Sometimes, it is okay to do what I want, even if it means someone's feelings might get hurt. I don't need to take every assignment or promotion offered. Nor do I have to do everything Opal wanted.* She flopped onto her stomach. *He was right about one thing. I don't always have to say yes.* She turned over, slipped to the edge of the bed, and dropped her feet to the floor.

She paced in front of her bed. *How do I stop doing everything for others and start doing a few things for myself?* After passing by her bedroom mirror for the third time, she hesitated. "First step." She pointed at her reflection. "Tell Opal you will not keep your promise." She frowned. *How would she react? Opal is a wonderful mom, but Kansas has a father, even if she doesn't admit it. Clay loves me, and I will not hide from him just because she says I should forget we ever met.*

Mel turned her head toward the noise on her nightstand. Her smile widened, and she grabbed the buzzing phone. Her smile faded. *Opal.*

—How did Kansas' last day of school go? Did you get pictures? Tell her I love and miss her.—

Mel sat on the edge of her bed, massaging her shoulders. She didn't need Opal to worry about anything other than staying safe. Mel sank her head onto the pillow. If she hadn't promised Opal not to see Clay, she'd tell her how he pushed Kansas on the swing, orchestrated the entire campfire party, and formed a bond with Kansas. She wanted to explain how Clay rushed her and Kansas to urgent care, even though they had broken up, and how she dismissed him, not because he wasn't good enough to love but because Opal demanded it. Instead, she told her about the sprained wrist and the program, omitting she had forgotten to take pictures. Guilt for not capturing this special moment tightened her throat. Excitement straightened her shoulders. Clay had taken quite a few shots, along with a video. She quickly texted, promising to send photos later.

She curled into a fetal position, clutching her pillow. *I should have told Opal, but I fell apart.* Shame sent the pillow flying across the room. Mel grabbed her phone.

—Clay, I miss you. Also, will you send me photos from the program today?—

He immediately responded.

—I can stop by with my phone, and you can scroll through and pick out the ones you want.—

Excitement rushed up her spine and sent shivers down her arms and legs. Before her inner chatter about keeping Opal's promise clouded her brain and changed her mind, she texted.

—The front door will be open.—

She jumped from the bed and stood in front of the mirror. "I am done going through life, making everyone happy at my expense." She threaded her fingers through her hair and marveled at her grinning reflection. "I should listen to you more often." Mel winked.

****

The following day, Mel hummed as she poured ground beans into the coffee machine. The rising sun splashing through the windowpane matched her mood, bright and filled with promise. She heard the floor creak and turned toward the doorway.

Clay's smile lit up his face and crinkled his eyes as he rushed over, wrapping his arms around her waist. "Morning, gorgeous." He nuzzled her neck.

"Good morning, Handsome." She turned slowly and pressed her lips to his. After a lingering kiss, she blushed. "Can I get you coffee?"

"*Hmm.*" He gazed into her eyes before releasing her. "Can't think of a better way to start the day."

She placed a cup on the counter before him and grabbed one for herself.

"Are you having second thoughts?" He brushed his fingertips across her forehead.

Hearing the concern in his voice, she shook her head. "Not about you." She took a long sip of coffee. "It's Opal. I still haven't told her you know Kansas is your daughter."

Clay raised his cup, blowing the rising steam from the surface. "Will her reaction change how you feel about me?"

"No, but my feelings for Kansas and Opal won't change, either. I've loved them a lot longer than I've loved you." She scrunched her face. *Why did he pop his mouth open and widen his gaze?* She formed the word, *oh*, before covering her mouth with her right hand. *I can't believe I just blurted the words out.*

"You love me?" He grinned and took a sip.

"Auntie," Kansas called out. "My arm itches. Help me take this off."

"Just a minute, honey." Mel stood.

Clay set his cup on the sink and leaned in close to Mel. "You love me? You love me."

With a flutter in her stomach and an urge to giggle and dance, she pulled him close. "I love you."

"How long have you known?" He winked and leaned back. "Before I go. Two things. First, I love you more. Second, your nightgown is inside out." He arched his eyebrows and widened his smile. "See ya." He turned and danced out the kitchen door.

Mel rested a hand over her fluttering heart and watched him leave.

"Auntie, are you coming?"

"Be there in a minute, sweetie." Mel rushed to put on clothes.

After settling Kansas in front of the TV with a bowl of cereal, she tossed in a load of laundry and started drafting a long list of things to do. By midmorning, she sat in the kitchen with another cup of coffee, wrestling with her conscience about whether to tell Opal.

"Auntie." Kansas stomped into the kitchen with the TV remote. "Saturdays are boring. Let's do something fun."

"Didn't you tell Uncle Clay you would water the flowers?"

She huffed and rolled her eyes. "That's not fun."

"Okay, I'll text Clay and let him know. I'm sure he can find someone else."

"No." She shook a finger at her chest. "I'm Uncle's helper. I'll give them a drink." She marched toward the kitchen door and paused. "Don't tell him to get a new helper. Please?"

"Okay." Mel sat at the kitchen table, enjoying her coffee as she texted Clay.

—Hey, Handsome, I'm drinking coffee and thinking about you while your helper is watering flowers.—

The phone vibrated immediately after sending her text. She glanced at the screen. *Clay.* She giggled as she read his text.

—Hey, Sunshine, I'm back from a run, and all I could think about was you. My best run ever.—

She re-read the text before cradling the phone against her chest. Mel floated through the rest of the day, allowing Kansas to stream movies while she exchanged dozens of texts.

Clay told her Gascon had passed the final building inspections and that he'd be in Kansas City for four or five days.

—I'll miss you as I contemplate how to handle my broken promise to Opal.—

—Remember, you and I are a team. If you want me to help, even to just hold your hand while you decide.—

—Thanks, Clay. I appreciate the offer, but I'll figure this out.—

Mel let Kansas celebrate the first day of her summer break with her favorite dinner foods: chicken nuggets, dinosaur cheesy macaroni, and chocolate pudding with whipped topping and sprinkles.

"Best meal ever." Kansas slid her chair away from the table. "I'm going to play a game on your tablet."

"Put your dishes in the dishwasher, and then you can play the game." Mel opened the cupboard and grabbed a couple of containers for leftovers.

The girl put one hand on her hip. "No."

"Kansas." She exhaled. "Put the dishes into the dishwasher."

"I don't want to." Kansas leaned closer. "You can't make me."

"Put your dishes." Mel pointed, sighing heavily. "In the dishwasher."

Kansas stomped. "I'm calling mom." She narrowed her gaze until she squinted. "She'll tell you I don't have to."

Mel picked the phone up off the counter, scrolled through the contacts to Opal, and put the phone on speaker. "Here you go, Kansas. Call your mom." She held out the phone.

Kansas grabbed the phone. She held her thumb over the call symbol. "Watch." She bobbed her head. "I'm doing it."

"Go ahead." She shrugged. "But you'll still put your dishes in the dishwasher before you play a game on my tablet."

Kansas waved the phone. "I'm calling."

"Hello? Is everything okay?" Opal shouted.

Mel stared at her niece and clenched her teeth to stop her from screaming. *What did you do?* The rapid beat of her heart pounded in her head. She hated lying to her sister, but now wasn't the time to reveal she had broken her promise.

"Hello," Opal repeated.

"Mom," Kansas wailed. "I don't want to put my dishes in the washer. My arm hurts. Auntie's being mean. I want to live with Uncle Clay."

"Turn off the speaker and give Auntie the phone."

"No. Come home. She's mean. I hate living with Auntie."

"Kansas, you'll do as I say," Opal commanded. "Hand Auntie the phone."

The phone sailed through the air, bounced off the wall, and landed in the kitchen sink. Kansas raced from the room, screaming, "Everyone is so mean!"

Mel listened to the sound of sandals slapping the hardwood floor. "Kansas! Don't run!" She stormed across the room and grasped the phone out of the sink. She rolled her eyes and swore softly at the black shattered screen. "Great. You broke the phone."

"What just happened?"

"Opal." Mel paced, sucking in large gulps of air as she gathered her thoughts.

"What's going on?"

"Nothing." She exhaled and continued in a steady voice, hoping Opal wouldn't hear her fear. She didn't want her to worry. "Everything's good." She swallowed down the truth. She cringed. *I just bought this phone.* "Kansas dropped the phone in the sink." She stared at the spiderweb of cracks on the black screen. *There's another eight hundred dollars wasted.* "Where's the speaker button?"

"How should I know? Maybe you need to take Kansas back to the doctor?"

Mel pushed the hair from her face. "The swelling is down; this is her first complaint." She cringed at the

119

sound of her squeaky high voice. *Did Opal think I'm neglecting Kansas?* "She has an appointment for a checkup."

"What's this about Clay? You promised you wouldn't see him."

Mel slumped against the counter, gasping. She tugged at the neckline of her shirt. "Yeah. Well, I bumped into him at work. None of this is a big deal. I needed a ride. You know Kansas is good. Kids act out. I shouldn't have given her the phone. Sorry, we bothered you."

"You're acting strange. You're a terrible liar. That's why I told you I don't want Clay near Kansas. You'll blab, or Clay will figure out he's Kansas' dad. She looks like him," Opal's voice echoed through the kitchen.

"What?" Kansas shouted.

"Is the speaker on?" Opal gasped.

"The screen is completely blank." Mel swallowed down the fear and tears. "I didn't know how to shut the—"

"Mel, what have you done?" Opal gasped. "Kansas, sweetheart," she purred. "Are you still there? Sweetheart?"

"Is Uncle my daddy?" Kansas placed her hands on her hips and moved closer to the phone. "My friends all know their daddy's name. Is my daddy's name Clay?"

"We can talk about this after I get home, sweetie," Opal murmured.

Mel clasped the phone tighter, moving closer to Kansas. She put a hand on her shoulder and mouthed, *it's okay*. Opal was the one who needed to fix things; the only thing she could do was comfort Kansas.

"Mommy, is Uncle Clay my daddy?" Kansas roared. "Mommy, is Uncle Clay my daddy?"

"Yes, sweetie." Opal's voice crackled through the speaker.

Kansas clapped her hands. "Thank you, thank you. Now, I have an Uncle Daddy."

"I love you, Kansas," Opal whimpered. "Sweetie, send me more pictures. I need to go to work. Momma loves you. Kisses and sweet dreams, baby."

Mel pressed her lips together. The desire to make another irrational promise was on the tip of her tongue, but she knew this wasn't her problem to fix. "Opal. Can you still hear me?" She looked at the shattered screen. "Opal?" She rummaged through the junk drawer for a charger and plugged in the silent phone. *Please work.* "Hello, Opal?"

The phone remained muted. No lights, no sound. She rubbed her stomach and swallowed down the sour taste in her mouth. *I should have told Opal about Clay. If she had, maybe this phone conversation wouldn't have happened. I've made a mess of everything. Opal is thousands of miles away and can't comfort her daughter.* Mel collapsed in a kitchen chair, staring at the wall. *The bright-yellow wall Opal had painted. I need to let Clay know, but how?*

"Auntie..." Kansas danced around the kitchen.

Mel exhaled, ignoring the chatter while rubbing the tension from her neck. *I need time to think.*

"I have an Uncle Daddy. I have an Uncle Daddy, and his name is Clay." Her feet stopped. "Auntie, what's wrong? Your face is funny."

Mel blinked away the storm of emotions raging inside her. Frustration at her inability to comfort Opal.

Anger because she couldn't call Clay. If only Kansas hadn't thrown the phone.

A small hand brushed her forearm. "I'm sorry. I'll put my dishes away."

Mel gave her a quick side hug as she gained control of her feelings. "Okay."

Five minutes later, Kansas sang, "All done, Auntie. Want to play a game?"

Mel used what little energy she had to nod. *How will I ever fix this mess?* She couldn't think of one solution. She zombie-walked through the remainder of the night. Her brain traveled at sloth speed. Mel walked into her bedroom. *Did I put Kansas to sleep or leave her on the sofa?* She retraced her steps and sighed at the sight of Kansas in her bed.

Back in her room, she slipped on her nightgown and flopped onto the mattress. She ran her hands across the sheet. *Clay.* She sniffed and could still smell a hint of cedar. She remembered his arms wrapped around her. Is this how Opal feels longing for her daughter? Is this how Kansas feels longing for two parents while stuck with her auntie? Mel tossed and turned and, at some point, fell asleep because she awoke to a jab. She could feel her neck muscles twitch, and she forced her eyelids open.

"Come on, Auntie. Wake up. I want to call my Uncle Daddy."

Mel grabbed the silent phone on her nightstand and handed it to Kansas.

She stared at the screen, her gaze widening as she tapped the cracked glass. "It won't turn on." She burst into tears. "I didn't mean to break it."

Mel sat and resisted the urge to tell her everything

would be fine. She needed to know consequences followed her actions.

"You could buy a new one." Kansas brushed her tears aside.

"Phones cost a lot of money."

"I have money. I'll be right back." She raced out of the bedroom.

Mel walked barefoot into the kitchen in her nightgown. The kitchen counter still had the remains from last night's supper. She sighed and started the coffee brewing.

Moments later, Kansas rushed to the counter with her cupped hands, and coins pinged off the floor. "Can we go get a phone now?"

"First, you need to eat breakfast and water the plants. I have a kitchen to clean and work emails to send."

"I want my Uncle Daddy." She stuck out her bottom lip. "Please. We can buy a phone and then work, please, Auntie."

Mel also wanted to talk to Clay, but Kansas would have a million excuses about why she couldn't help once they had a phone. "First, breakfast. I'll have my coffee, and we'll clean and water before we get a phone."

Just short of noon, they had completed their chores, slipped into the car, and started driving to the store.

"Auntie, can you buy me a cell phone, too?"

Mel glanced in the rearview mirror. "No." She clamped her jaw tight to keep in the words. *No how and no way am I buying you a phone.*

The large plate-glass windows advertised the latest phones with a limited-time offer. Mel opened the heavy door.

A teenage boy sighed and half-heartedly pointed to a display. "Take a number."

She scanned the store and counted ten people. "How long is the wait?"

He shrugged. "Take a number." He pointed again.

A couple rushed around Kansas and grabbed a number.

That's my number. She grabbed Kansas' hand and raced forward to take number twenty-nine before anyone else barged ahead. At first, she and Kansas busied themselves checking out the phones and choosing the prettiest color and fanciest case.

But after the third lap around the store, Kansas crossed her arms over her chest. "I'm bored."

Mel leaned against a display counter, shifting from side to side. "Me, too."

"I'm hungry." Kansas tugged on Mel's hand. "Can we go eat?"

"We can, but we won't have a phone. We'll only have this number." Mel flipped the paper over and over.

"That's okay." Kansas tugged her toward the door.

"We can't call anyone."

Kansas loosened her grip. "Okay. Auntie, do you have any gum in your purse?"

Mel dug. *Please let there be at least a couple of cough drops.* She scooped out empty wrappers and tissue dust. "Sorry, sweetie. Nothing to eat."

"It's okay." She patted her stomach.

Mel shook her head. *When I saw the line, why didn't I leave? Love.* She grinned. *Clearly, I'm not thinking straight. Letting Kansas go hungry because I don't want to go a day without talking to Clay.* She grabbed Kansas' hand. "Let's go get something to eat before we both starve." *I need to get a grip on my emotions.*

Chapter Twelve

On Monday, Mel stepped into the kitchen and ruffled Kansas' hair. "You're up early. Don't suppose you made coffee?"

"Auntie, you're silly. But I made my breakfast." She tapped her spoon on the overflowing bowl of Honey Ohs. "I'm telling Alyssa I have an Uncle Daddy. And all day, we get to play."

Half listening, Mel nodded. *If someone asks about Clay, what should I say? Is he my boyfriend or my sister's baby daddy?* She practiced several responses as she packed Kansas' lunch. *Yes, I'm dating my niece's father.* Mel smiled as she replaced the school papers in Kansas' backpack with sunscreen, a beach towel, fruit snacks, and a spare change of clothes.

Mel checked her laptop one last time for an email from Opal, but the only personal email messages were advertisements and spam. *Is Opal upset because I'm in love with Clay? Does Clay harbor feelings for Opal? Will Kansas want Mom and Dad to live together?*

"Come on, Auntie. I want to go."

After a last peek at her email, she followed Kansas to the car. Mel couldn't keep up with her thoughts, and drove on autopilot to the day care summer program. She stopped at the drop-off area instead of parking in the lot.

When the car stopped, Kansas kicked the back door

open with her feet. "My friends are here." She scampered out of the car, dragging her backpack across the sidewalk as she ran to the girls and the child care attendant.

"Well, good-bye then. Have fun." Mel waved, her thoughts shifting to work and the deadline for testing their new software. Today, they'd be working from the fourth floor. Would Clay still be there? She smiled, wet her lips, and sped off.

Mel searched for Clay's truck in Gascon's parking lot. *He's not here.* She exhaled. Weighed down by longing and the need to tell him, she dragged her feet across the parking lot. *What if he thinks I'm ghosting him?* Panic bubbled from her stomach as she slumped through the employees' entrance and took the stairs up four flights. *This is not the way I wanted to start the week.* Panting, she pushed through the door and squinted at the sunlight shining through the windows. At the pungent smell of paint and new carpet, she wrinkled her nose. Everything looked crisp and clean, like spring after a long, harsh winter. She forced a smile. "Good morning." She waved. "Welcome to your new home."

A couple of her team members glanced over, but most only grunted as their gazes remained fixated on boxes.

She entered her small office, and on her new desk sat red and yellow tulips. *Are these flowers from Clay? Maybe he misses me. Goose bumps crawled across her forearms. Or is he having second thoughts and wants space?* She rushed forward and plucked the card from the arrangement.

What should we name our team? Love, Clay.

The heaviness vanished, and the smile on her lips turned genuine. She twirled, hugging the card to her chest, but the sudden appearance of Paula in her doorway stilled her steps. The ambiguity of the question tightened her grip. *She'll want to know the meaning.*

"Let me see that." Paula strode over and wrestled the card from Mel's fingers. "What kind of question is that? Is he asking his name, your name, or a hyphenated name?" A slow smile settled on Paula's face as she hummed. *Dum-dum-da-dum, dum-dum-da-dum.*

"An inside joke." Mel pushed the hair from her flushed face. *Does Paula know something I don't?*

"A girl can wish." Paula held out a large cup of coffee. "Hopefully, you're ready because your calendar is full, honey. Welcome to Monday."

Paula had underestimated the number of scheduled meetings. If Leo hadn't canceled the two o'clock, then Mel wouldn't have had time to go to the bathroom and send a quick email to Opal. Hoping to erase her fears, she included an anecdote about Kansas' excitement at telling her friends about her daddy. But then hit Delete and only mentioned she hadn't replaced her phone. That things were busy at work and she'd let her know when she got a new one. After hitting Send, she buried her face in her hands. *What will I do if we don't reconcile?*

****

The rest of Monday and all of Tuesday became a blur of meetings, emails, and software testing failures. Mel had no chance to purchase a phone. But today was Wednesday, and Paula had blocked off her morning so she could purchase a phone. *I wonder how many missed messages I'll have from Clay.*

Kansas walked into the kitchen, stuffing the head of her sleepy-eyed doll into her backpack. "Come on, Auntie, I want to see my friends, and don't forget to buy a phone. I need to tell Uncle Daddy about day camp."

Pouring the rest of her coffee into a to-go cup, she nodded, grabbed two fruit snacks, and locked the door behind Kansas. *I have so much to tell him, too.* Mel stood beside her car in the driveway and shifted her gaze to the ground. She watched her feet sink slowly into the soggy grass. Kansas had left the hose on overnight *again.* She stomped onto the driveway pavement. *My feet will stink like a swamp monster.* "Thanks for watering the flowers, Kansas."

"You're welcome, Auntie."

"Hurry and shut the water off." She drew her eyebrows together. How had Kansas escaped the expanding marsh around the front bush? As she tapped her left shoe and watched the water drip off, she spotted an envelope pinned by her windshield wiper. "What now?" Mel bit her lip to keep from cursing and scanned the surrounding area. *Who put something on my windshield? Did someone report me for allowing her to over-water?*

Kansas ran back. "Auntie, are you in trouble?" She stretched her neck. "Did you get sent home with a note?"

She waved the contents of the red envelope. "Four tickets to Saturday's MN Twinkles Game!" *How long have these been here? Clay.* Her arms ached. *I want to hug him, hear his voice whispering in my ear...run my fingers through his hair...and smell his cedar aftershave. If only I could text him.* Sighing, she climbed into the car.

Mel dropped Kansas off at her summer program and repeated it for the tenth time. "Yes, Kansas." She stooped to tell her good-bye. "I'll get a phone, and tonight, you can call Clay."

"My Uncle Daddy."

Fifteen minutes later, she stood outside the cellular store and watched through the glass door as a young woman unlocked the front door. Mel rushed inside. And what should have been a quick transaction turned into a problem.

The young clerk shook her head while attempting to transfer the phone's data. "Hmm, let me check your SIM card. The data transfer won't work." The clerk shrugged. "I'll have to restore your backup to the new phone."

"A backup! I don't have a backup." Mel raised her hands and then dropped her arms in defeat. *I feel like I just set off the exit alarm at an upscale jewelry store.* "The phone is only a few months old."

The clerk stared wide-eyed, her mouth gaping and her gold tongue piercing visible.

"Yeah, yeah. I'm stupid." Mel brushed the hair from her face.

"We could try a data recovery. But there is no guarantee all your messages and contacts will be salvageable."

"Okay. But what about texts I haven't read? Can I recover any unread texts from the weekend?"

She shook her head. "Sorry. All carriers purge their cycle after thirty-six to forty-eight hours. So, no texts or missed calls from the weekend."

The clerk sounded like the sped-up disclaimer on a TV ad. "Okay, do the data recovery." Mel left the store, scanning her contacts. Opal and most of her work contact information had transferred, but day care, Clay's, and doctor's numbers had disappeared.

At work, she entered all but one of her missing contacts. Clay's. She sighed. *No way will I go downstairs and ask Bill for the information. He'd ask why and maybe report me to Human Resources.* Even though she had done nothing wrong, the thought sent a shiver down her spine.

Maybe Clay will text. But the only messages she received came from employees. *Does he think I'm ghosting him?* She could feel her chest tighten. If he ignored my texts and calls, I'd be pounding on his door, but he didn't fight for Liz. He might not fight for me, either.

"Hey." Paula rushed through the doorway.

Mel clutched her chest. "You scared the daylight out of me. I can't hear you coming down the carpeted hallway. Put bells on your shoes, knock, or something."

"So, honey, how many texts did Tall, Dark, and Lonesome send?"

She grimaced and repeated the store clerk's disclaimer about purged message cycles. "What will I do if he doesn't call? If I had known his number wouldn't transfer—I would have gotten—I don't know. Should I send him a fruit basket and include an explanation? Paula, help me fix this."

"A big hunk of a man gives you four tickets to the MN Twinkles game, and your first thought is sending a basket of fruit to his house?" Paula puckered her face and drew her eyebrows together. "Didn't he tell you he'd be out of town for a few days? I don't think coming home to a basket of furry mangoes and black bananas on his doorstep will flip the switch you're hoping for."

"I don't even have his business card. Do you have his number?" Mel stood. "Please say *yes*."

"You think this is the nineties, and I have a rotary file of business cards? Seriously?" Paula tapped a finger on her chin. "But I have their business number. I'll call the company and say he forgot something at Gascon, and when they ask, what? I could say he forgot you."

Mel shook a finger at Paula. "Absolutely, no. Besides being inappropriate, you'd embarrass me. Okay, he left me the tickets on my windshield. So, I'll drive by his house and put something on his vehicle. No, that won't work. He parks his truck in the garage. I'll put something in his mailbox. I'll stop by the store and get a card. Thanks." She sat and wiped her wet palms against her slacks.

"No problem. I ordered lunch for the team, and you meet at one in conference room four."

After work, Mel gasped at the sight of Kansas. She brushed the curls from the dirt-smeared face. "Did you get a mud facial?"

"Huh, Auntie?" She yawned. "We spent all day digging for dinosaurs and didn't find one bone."

One look at her niece, and Mel knew that getting a card and dropping it off was out of the question. She needed to get Kansas home. After a quick dinner and a bath, she tucked Kansas into bed and gave her a goodnight kiss on her sleepy face.

Her eyes closed, she mumbled, "Uncle Daddy, tell you…"

Will you dream of Uncle Daddy? Mel brushed the curls from her neck. How tough to be a six-year-old girl and find out your daddy lived and played in the same neighborhood, and now she can't even call him because we don't have his stupid phone number. Mel returned to her home office and slumped into the chair. She rubbed her eyes before seeing an email from Opal. Trembling, she pushed the mouse to open the correspondence. *Am I forgiven?*

I'm in the field for the rest of the week. Big kisses for Kansas.

She swallowed. *Opal is still angry.* The tension in her shoulders knotted her muscles. *Can Opal focus on her mission when she's worried about Kansas and angry at me? If anything happens, I'll never forgive myself.* She pushed the thoughts aside and kneaded the pain in her left shoulder. Even though she knew Opal was an adult and needed to address the issue with Clay, she couldn't deny doubts lingered. *I disappointed her, and I don't know how to make things better.*

With no solutions coming to mind, she shifted her focus to work. Fifteen minutes later, a flashing ad on the sidebar caught her attention. Edible flower arrangements. *Perfect for Clay.* She only needed to complete the card to place an order, but she wasn't sure what to say. She wanted to explain everything, but they had a limit of twenty-five characters.

—*Tel brkn. Pls call.*—

After a quick web search, she added the text code for *I love you, today, tomorrow, and forever*.

—*831 224*—

Thursday dragged, and at dinner, Kansas shoved her carrots and peas into her mashed potatoes and planted her spoon in the middle. "When is Uncle Daddy coming over? Why doesn't he call?" Kansas repeated her question all night, as if a different answer would come.

"I don't know Kansas. Clay's out of town. He's busy with work." For each of Kansas' questions, Mel added another excuse to the answer. She checked on her package and sighed. The date of delivery had changed to Friday by four.

"Auntie, I'm bored. Let's go to the park."

Mel popped up from the kitchen chair. "Great idea, kiddo. Hurry." She tossed the remains of supper into the sink and raced to the bedroom. After changing into a scoop-neck pink shirt and a denim skirt, she stood in front of her mirror. Just-kissed lips—check, Misty Evening perfume—check, winning smile—check. "All right, girl, don't fail me now."

****

After an hour at the park, Mel pushed her damp hair behind her ear and shook out her achy arms. "Three more pushes."

"Auntie, it's okay." Kansas dragged her toes into the dirt and stopped the swing. "I'm tired, too. Can we go home?"

"Of course, kiddo." They walked home in silence.

Friday night was a repeat of Thursday, and once again, she walked Kansas home in silence, disappointed she hadn't seen Clay.

Kansas kicked her shoes off at the door. "Auntie?"

"Yes, Kansas." Mel locked the front door behind them.

"Maybe Uncle Daddy broke his phone, and he lost our number."

She gathered Kansas against her chest. "I think you're right." *How tough to find your daddy only to lose him. I will give him until Sunday, and if I don't hear from him, I'm marching over to his house and demanding an explanation.*

****

On Saturday morning, Mel walked by her bedroom mirror and snarled. "You lost your man. You let everyone at work boss you around. And you haven't told Opal what's in your heart." She grimaced at her reflection. "Kansas," she called from her bedroom closet and forced a smile. "Come help me pick out something to wear to the game."

"Okay." Kansas skipped into the closet and twirled in her new MN Twinkles shirt. "Auntie. You, too, have a new shirt. We match. We're Twinzies. The tooth fairy is silly. Why does she bring shirts for loose teeth and leave money for lost teeth?"

Mel smiled. "I don't know, but there are two more shirts. One for Alyssa and another for McKenzie. Twinzies, eh? Why didn't I think of that?"

Kansas tried to clap, but the arm brace made a hollow thud. She stomped her feet and cheered. "Yay. Can we go? I want to show them our matching shirts."

"Sure can." She reached up to massage her achy cheeks from forcing a smile. Outside, not a cloud was in the sky—perfect weather for a late afternoon game with temperatures in the low seventies.

****

Mel tugged the hem of her damp shirt. *What was I thinking, taking three kids? I should have invited Paula.* "Come on. Everyone hold hands. Remember. We all stay together," she repeated as she snuck the three girls

135

past the sweet aroma of cotton candy, the buttery bliss of freshly popped corn, and masses of jumbo jug sodas. Mel allowed the girls to stop and pick up three lemonades before moving them forward by promising gummy animals and fruity snacks once everyone sat in their seats.

They marched down ten rows of stairs before finding the correct row. Mel released a sigh of relief. With the girls sandwiched between two robust middle-aged women on the left side and Mel on the right, the kids couldn't escape.

The women fawned over the appearance of three miniature-sized MN Twinkles.

After the fourth inning, she counted. One, two, three. She exhaled. So far, so good. The girls shared a cotton candy and now munched on roasted peanuts. The women, on the other end, did not mind sharing. *Oh well, as long as no one goes home with woozy stomachs or sticky hair.*

Mel rubbed her stomach and took another sip of water as she listened to the girls giggling. At least, they're enjoying themselves. She heard her phone buzz. Every nerve hummed with anticipation. *Paula.* She sighed. *Is Clay ever going to respond?*

—*Have you lost anyone yet?*—

As the MN Twinkles waited for the ground crew to finish dragging along the home stretch, Mel stood and took a photo of the girls sitting with their handfuls of peanuts and sent the picture to Paula. She placed her hands on her lower back, stretched, and turned to watch the fans. *Clay.* She blinked. *He's back in town! Why didn't he call, text, or drive over?*

Wrinkles creased his forehead.

The greeting she wanted to shout stuck in her throat, and instead of waving, she swiped her cold, damp palms against her thighs. *Why doesn't he wave or shout hello? Will he ask me to hand over Kansas?*

He stopped beside the vacant seat.

Mel turned her body to shield Kansas from his grasp. *I won't let her go.* She could feel her muscles stiffen until she stood like a guard outside a palace.

"Uncle Daddy," Kansas squealed.

Mel blocked her niece from rushing to him.

"Uncle Daddy." She shook the bag of peanuts like a pompom.

He's not taking Kansas. Mel clenched her jaw.

Clay smiled, and his left dimple appeared. "Hello." His left eyebrow arched as he stepped next to Mel.

Did he set this up to see me? Why hadn't he called or come over? He's up to something. She drew her brows together as she continued to study him.

"So." He sat in the vacant seat. He tapped his fingers against his thigh and tilted his head. "Eight-three-one-two-two-four isn't your new phone number."

Mel swallowed. "Oh, the numbers represent—" She dropped into the chair. "I only had twenty-five characters to add a message." *What if he no longer feels the same way?* She twisted her hands together.

"Maybe one of the kids can tell me."

After glancing over and seeing his amusement, she realized she had gotten wound up with worry over nothing. She leaned closer. "I love you today, tomorrow, and forever. The first letter of each word is the—"

"I've missed you." His words rushed against her ear as he wrapped an arm around her.

"Those are my other three favorite words." She gazed into his eyes, forgetting about her niece and friends, as her fears melted like snow on a hot spring day. "I've missed you, too." She could feel the tension from the last few days puddle harmlessly around her feet.

"Auntie!" Kansas screamed. "Auntie, you and Uncle Daddy are on the TV."

Mel shifted her gaze to the screen, expecting the big heart-shaped kiss camera, but the screen flashed.

Marry Me, Mel.

Oh my. She placed a hand on her rumbling heart. *Clay is proposing.* Goose bumps shivered up and down her arms. *He wants to marry me.* She glanced over. *Was this a joke or a mistake?*

He shifted from his seat and knelt, holding a stunning pearl-and-diamond ring. "Our first kiss was right here at this stadium. When our lips parted, I knew you were the one woman for me. You're the one I want to spend the rest of my life with. With you, I only see possibilities. Mel, will you marry me?"

Tears streamed from her eyes, and she opened her mouth. "Yes, yes, yes."

He slid the promise of happily ever after onto her left ring finger.

Mel kissed him, wetting both their cheeks with her tears.

The crowd cheered wildly.

Kansas and her friends giggled and threw peanuts all over them.

Mel smiled, and as much as she loved baseball, she continually shifted her gaze between Clay and her ring. She pushed away the urge to call her sister and share the exciting news. *How can I marry Clay without Opal's blessing?*

"You, okay?" Clay slid an arm around her shoulders.

"Yes. Perfect." *I am going to marry Clay and get Opal's blessing, but how?*

Chapter Thirteen

After the baseball game, Mel drove Kansas' friends to their homes. She pulled into the driveway and smiled as Clay parked his truck beside her. Outside, she stood next to him as the evening sky turned bright-orange and yellow.

He kissed her twice before leaning back. "Did you drop Kansas off somewhere?"

"No, she's in the car, but she might need help to get out of her seat with the wrist brace."

Clay opened the back door. "She's asleep." He unbuckled the seat and shifted her into his arms. "I think I'm supposed to carry you across the door."

"That's on our wedding night, but if you want to practice, I can wait until you get her to bed." Mel slapped a mosquito. "Second thought, I'm coming inside. The bugs will eat me alive."

"Fine, but you'll disappoint Paula with your unromantic behavior."

Mel sighed at the sweet sight of him carrying his daughter into her room. She tiptoed closer, standing outside the door as he tucked her into bed. She overheard him wishing her a good night. Like eating ice cream too fast, the warmth switched to pain. Opal has gone to bed for almost a year, knowing someone else was kissing Kansas good night. *Did she make me promise not to see Clay, because she felt guilty? Has*

140

this deployment made her realize she made a mistake in depriving Clay of the *opportunity to see his daughter? Or is Opal worried she'll lose custody of Kansas because she isn't here to parent?*

Minutes later, Mel stood next to him in the hall. "I can't believe—When? How—"

Clay silenced her attempts at words with his kisses.

She leaned into his embrace, drawing him closer, until she could feel his beating heart.

"You said yes."

"I did. And I do." Mel grinned. "This all happened so fast." She raised her left hand and gazed at the pearl and diamond ring. "It's beautiful. I've seen nothing like it. Where did you get it?"

"The ring is the reason I left town. The wedding ring belonged to my grandmother. She wanted me to remember to live my life with no regrets. After Kansas fell and sprained her wrist, and then you nearly passed out in my arms, I needed to let you know what I felt in my heart. When my texts and calls went unanswered, I regretted not asking you to be my wife. I meant every word when I said we are a team, partners, friends, and…" His husky voice faltered. "Lovers."

Mel rested her right hand over her heart. "I have always been sensible and serious, and you make me giddy. That is just one of many things I love about you. But…" She placed her head on his chest and heard his heartbeat slow down.

"But," he repeated.

"Opal and I are sisters." The words gushed between broken breaths. "She has missed out on so much this year. I want her to be happy for us. I love you, Clay, but I can't imagine Opal coming home and finding out I got engaged. Besides, I haven't told her we're officially back together."

They swayed to the beat of a sad, silent, broken lover's ballad. She slipped the ring off her finger. "Will you hold on to the ring until I work things out with Opal?"

Clay rubbed a thumb across the pearl. "Did I rush this?"

"Everything's perfect. The only hesitation is Opal." She leaned into him. Their lips met. *I hope he feels all the love in my heart.* She tightened her grasp around his waist.

He leaned back and sighed. "It's not what I wanted to hear, but I understand. I want to tell my family and friends about us getting married, but we can wait. Family is important to me. And that's another thing I love about you. Family first." He slipped the ring into his pocket. "The only thing I want more than you for my wife is for you to be happy."

Their lips met in a tender, sweet kiss.

"Hey." He brushed his thumb beneath her chin. "I'm going home, but I'll return in the morning. We can all have breakfast together."

"Clay."

"Shh, everything will be okay. We will figure this out."

After locking the door and turning out the lights, she crawled into bed. Her arms ached with the desire to hold him. *Did I make a mistake? Should I have kept the ring and hoped Opal understood? How can I live without regrets if I put everyone's happiness ahead of mine?*

****

Buzz-buzz-buzz.

On Sunday morning, Mel woke with a start. She swept her gaze around the room before grabbing her ringing phone. "Hello?"

"Good morning, gorgeous. I'm at your front door. Want to let me in?"

"Of course, Clay. I'll be right there." Mel jogged to the door in her nightgown, slid back the lock, and threw open the door. "Wow. Good-looking." She tangled her fingers in his T-shirt as she beckoned him inside.

"You're in a good mood. Sleeping late agrees with you. Hmm, I bet your bed is still warm." His gaze motioned toward the bedroom.

"We could check."

"Uncle Daddy." Kansas' feet echoed across the hall floor. "Auntie, I'm hungry. Can we eat?"

"Okay, team." Clay clapped his hands. "Mel, you make coffee. Kansas, you're in charge of toast, and I'll make the scrambled eggs."

Mel stood by the coffeemaker. The machine gurgled and sputtered before dripping the last drop of coffee into the pot. She inhaled the steamy scent of freshly brewed coffee before taking her first tentative sip. She took a longer drink and studied her team through the fragrant steam. *Will Clay still be eager to come over after Kansas returns home with Opal?* She washed away her fear with a long swig of coffee.

Kansas' eyebrows arched as they ate, and her mouth opened wide. "Auntie." She jumped. Her chair tilted backward and almost toppled. She ran around the table. "Auntie, your ring." Her small fingers pried Mel's hand apart. "It's gone." She blinked. "Last night, Uncle Daddy gave you a ring, and now? Did you lose it?"

Why did all the conversations seem to get harder? "No, silly, I didn't lose the ring. Clay is holding onto the ring for a while longer."

"Why?" Kansas bunched up her facial features.

"It's one of those complicated adult things." Mel took a sip of coffee and glanced at her naked third finger. She swallowed the bitterness. "Go finish your eggs before they get cold."

Kansas slunk back into her chair. She propped her elbow onto the table and rested her cheek against her fist. "Uncle Daddy, do you know why she isn't wearing the ring? I'd wear the ring."

He leaned closer to Kansas. "It's one of those complicated adult things."

"Oh." She scrunched her face.

"Sweetie." Mel set her empty cup at the center of the table. "Part of the adult thing that makes this complicated is we can't tell your mom about the ring. Okay?"

Kansas turned her head to Clay and then back to Mel. "Okay. Can you teach me to ride a bike today? Alyssa can ride without training wheels. I'm the only one who can't."

The bike had been sitting unused in the garage for almost a year. Guilt for not thinking to teach her how to ride it had her wanting to say *yes*. She shook her head. "As soon as you get your brace off. You can practice."

"Please, Auntie." Kansas lifted her glass. "I'll be careful. See, I can hold things. Please."

Mel shifted her gaze to Clay.

Please, he mouthed.

He had already missed her first steps, words,

starting school, and birthdays. "Okay, Clay can teach you after you brush your teeth and pick up your room."

She hovered, half standing and half sitting, above her chair. "Yes, Auntie."

After connecting with Kansas' gaze, she lowered her voice. "Don't stuff your dirty clothes and toys under your bed or in your closet. Put them where they belong. Dirty clothes in the hamper. Toys in your toy chest. Okay?"

"I'm going to ride a bike." She sang, scrambling as she raced to put her plate and cup in the dishwasher.

Mel stood. "I'll clean up the kitchen."

Clay wrapped an arm around her waist and kissed her neck tenderly. "Sit," he whispered. "I'll get you another coffee and clean up the dishes." After starting the dishwasher, he sat and joined her. "So, do you plan to spend the day tempting me in your nightgown, or will you get dressed?"

"Not until I finish my last sip."

"Can I get Opal's address?" Clay took a white envelope from his pocket. "She doesn't need to be worrying about custody battles and attorneys. Maybe this letter will put her mind at ease. I plan to be a part of Kansas' life, but we can discuss arrangements after she gets home. There's also a check to help cover child care expenses."

She found Opal's contact information and slid the phone before Clay. *He's a good man.* Swallowing down the sudden lump, she backed away from the table and pointed down the hall to the bathroom. Mel stood under the hot water in the shower and let her tears fall. *Opal is my sister, and I can't even find the courage to ask for her forgiveness. What's wrong with me?* She didn't have to think long about the question. *I lack courage.*

By lunch, Kansas gave up riding a bike. "I can't do it." She sat in a chair with her bottom lip quivering.

Mel rubbed her back. "Did I tell you about the time I taught your mom to ride?"

Kansas shook her head.

"Hmm." Mel brushed the curls from Kansas' eyes as Clay leaned closer. "All day, I hung onto the backseat of her bike and ran with her. Whenever I let go, boom! Down she went. We practiced after the streetlights turned on and everyone went home. My legs were like cooked spaghetti noodles.

" 'One more time,' your mom said.

"I held her up and ran.

"She yelled, 'Let go.'

"I did. Boom! Down she went, and I quit. All night, the rain fell. The next morning, your mom was determined to try again. But the sidewalks had big muddy puddles, and my legs hurt." Mel walked to the counter. She grabbed three plates and set them next to a loaf of bread.

Kansas tugged on her shirt. "What happened next?"

"I told her *no*. I didn't want to get wet and muddy running through puddles." She unscrewed the lid from a jar of peanut butter.

"So, my mom never learned to ride a bike?" Kansas put the bread on the plates.

"Your mom cried and cried, 'Please, please.' Finally, I gave in, and we walked the bike to an empty parking lot with only one giant puddle in the middle. Remember your pool party?"

Kansas widened her gaze. "Yeah, the biggest pool

ever."

"That's how big this puddle was." Mel spread the peanut butter onto the bread. "I held onto the backseat. 'Stay out of the water. Steer to the edge of the lot,' I said. 'Okay,' she screamed. 'Promise you won't let go until I tell you to.' She pedaled faster and faster toward the puddle. Her front wheel hit the water, and I let go." Mel threw her arms toward the ceiling.

"Oh, no." Kansas slapped her cheeks. "She wasn't ready. You let go too soon. Did my mom fall? Did she have to swim back?"

"Nope, she pedaled faster, throwing water high into the air. The spray shot out of her back wheel like a rooster's tail. Then she turned and rode back through the rippling water with a big smile."

Kansas folded her arms across her chest and pouted. "If I had a puddle, I could learn to ride."

"Your mom learned to ride a bike because she didn't quit trying, and I let go. Who's ready for lunch?"

When the time came to put Kansas to bed, she had the same smile her mother wore when riding through the puddle.

After Clay tucked Kansas into bed, he joined Mel on the sofa. The MN Twinkles played on the TV. He slid an arm over her shoulder and drew her to his chest. "Thanks for the story earlier. I'm unsure if the recap of teaching your sister to ride was for my benefit or for Kansas. Did you really teach Opal to ride a bike?"

"Yep, true story. Although, instead of a couple of days, we practiced for more than a week. She cried every morning until I caved and took her to practice. That is the sole reason I hate running and exercising, even today. Opal also cried at night because she couldn't ride the bike. My mom worked nights and slept days, and when Dad heard Opal fussing about the bike, he would come undone. So, I tried to keep her quiet."

Clay tensed. "Was he abusive?"

"No, but instead of a spanking, he used silence to punish us. Sometimes, he could go a month without saying a thing. When Mom heard me complaining, she'd tell us we were lucky. Every day, she treated kids whose dads burned them with cigarettes, broke their arms, or worse. She'd tell us to be happy. He fed us and provided a safe home. But as hard as I tried, I just couldn't feel grateful. I'd go to bed thinking about those kids and how our dad didn't like us."

"Is that why you don't want to send Opal a letter? Do you still need to protect her? Or do you still feel you need to keep her quiet?"

As Mel considered his question, she sucked in a deep breath and exhaled. "She pleaded and begged me not to see you. On the night Kansas found out you're her dad, Opal sounded so hurt and distraught. Of course, I'm protective of my baby sister. And I worry she won't forgive me for making her deployment more difficult."

He drew slow, lazy circles on her right arm with his thumb. "If you never ask, you'll never know. Maybe you need to let go, too."

She rested her head against his shoulder. "It'd be easier if she wasn't six thousand miles away. I miss her. I don't want to lose her."

His lips brushed her forehead with a kiss.

Is Clay right? Should I let go?

Chapter Fourteen

On Monday morning, Mel rubbed the sleep from her eyes and grabbed her buzzing phone from the nightstand. *Clay?* Her smile vanished. *Paula, what does she want?*

—Hey, Boss Lady, did you receive the latest email? 8 a.m. meeting with Leo and some executives from Texas. Welcome to Monday—

Mel scrambled out of her nightgown. "Kansas!" she yelled. "Get dressed." A hasty search in her closet produced black slacks and a cream-colored shirt. *I don't even have time for a shower.* She combed her hair back and secured the haphazard ponytail with a binder. She brushed her teeth, spritzed on cologne, and called down the hall. "Hurry, kiddo, I'm late."

When she didn't find her in the kitchen, she rushed into the bedroom. "Kansas." Mel stepped next to the bed. "Get up." She flipped the covers off. "I have an early morning meeting. Come on."

"I'm tired. My arm hurts." Kansas waved her right arm.

"Funny, but you sprained your left arm. Let's go."

"Oh." She blinked.

Mel held up a shirt.

Kansas raised her arms.

She is six years old and still wants me to dress her. She tugged the shirt over her head, slipped shorts over her legs, and tugged on socks. "Hurry." She shoved Kansas toward the bathroom. "I'll get your backpack. You can eat breakfast in the car."

As Mel drove into the day care parking lot, the low-fuel alarm beeped. *Can anything else go wrong?* She ran to the back door to get a sleeping Kansas and a half-eaten jelly toast out of her backseat. "Come on, honey." Mel did her best to unbuckle her while avoiding the grape jelly. She placed the remains of the breakfast on the roof of her car. "Sleepyhead, we're at day care. Let's go."

They walked hand in hand to the door. Inside, Mel stooped down. "Have a good day." She brushed a kiss across her cheek, turned, and ran back in her high heels. When she slipped behind the wheel, she noticed her shoes resembled combat boots, and the heels wobbled like stilts. The tires screeched out of the day care parking lot, and when her car jerked to a halt in Gascon's parking lot, she checked the time—eight fifteen.

Mel rushed through the lobby and didn't wait for the elevator. She took the stairs to the second floor and hobbled into the conference room with her right shoe in her left hand. She could feel her stomach drop faster than a sinker tossed by Duran at Saturday's baseball game as she stepped into the room. Mr. Hornet loomed larger-than-life in his alligator cowboy boots, dark denim pants, and a plaid shirt with pearl buttons. His black hair was shot through with threads of silver, and today, his white cowboy hat sat on the conference table.

"Glad you could make it," Mr. Hornet said.

She acknowledged his sarcasm with a slight curve of her upper lip and slipped into the vacant leather chair at the far end of the conference room. She swung her foot and tried squeezing her sore toes into the shoe. After a quick scan of the room, she squirmed and brushed a hand across her stomach. She tried to swallow. Texas had sent four executives to the meeting. She smiled and hoped the attention would go back to Mr. Hornet. The sound of rustling papers drew Mel's attention. She glanced across the table at her boss, Leo.

Mr. Hornet cleared his throat and narrowed his gaze at Leo.

"Sorry for the interruption." Leo slid the memo along the surface, and the rustle of the paper echoed off the silent walls.

Mel grasped the page, smiled, and nodded, hoping everyone would think this was old news. As she scanned the document for the second time, she let Mr. Hornet's words fade to background noise. *What?* She flashed her gaze back to Leo.

He beamed as he flashed a thumbs-up.

She bit down on her tongue. *Why isn't he outraged?* The new software rollout was on July fifteenth instead of November first. *The timeline is unrealistic. Even if they had written code, they'd still need additional testing time.* She glanced around the table and only saw a sea of agreement.

Mr. Hornet droned on. "...Shareholders will be happy. A win-win."

She shifted her gaze to Leo. *He looks like Texas' biggest supporter.* She swallowed down the sour bile rising in her throat. *Even if I could talk everyone into eighty-hour weeks and we had the code, the timeline would be nearly impossible.* The last time she checked, the coders still had issues, and she had already approved the summer vacation schedule. Mel cleared her throat and looked across the table.

Leo frantically shook his head and mouthed, *no*.

She swallowed down her objections. Leo must have a solution. Texas didn't fly up to Minnesota. *But they did. Why?* She watched Mr. Hornet lower his eyebrows and eyelids until his brown eyes were only slits. *Because they want everyone to buy into their plan and implement it.*

He stared.

Sweat pooled under her arms, and she resisted tugging at her shirt. She could almost hear Hornet say. *Hey, Mel, darling, don't bother kicking a bull after he's thrown you. Dust yourself off and run along.*

"Y'all have questions?" He smiled and looked around the room. His pointy-toed cowboy boots *click-clacked* as he paced in front of the room. "None." He pursed his lips. "Good. Good. Good." He flashed a bigger smile. "Everyone's on board." He *clicked-clacked* to the door and vanished like the great Oz behind the curtain.

Everyone started talking at once.

"Hey, Bob, did you get out golfing this weekend?"

"Leo, did I see you drive in with a new company truck?"

"Man, Leo, that's a sweet corporate vehicle. Where do I sign up?"

Mel pointed toward the memo. "Leo, do you have a moment?"

"Yeah, catch me after lunch." He stepped out and left Mel standing alone in the conference room.

No one invited me to lunch; it must only be for the senior leaders. The phone vibrated in her hand as she walked down the hall, and she slowed enough to read the message. *Clay.* She dropped her shoulders and took a deep breath.

—*Thinking about you.*—

He's so sweet. Another text.

—*Do you want to do dinner tonight?*—

Her smile faded. *How can I manage seeing Clay, spending time with Kansas, and ensuring my team meets this ridiculous time limit?* She balled her hands into fists, wanting to punch something. This wasn't fair. *How can they expect me to tell my team summer vacations are canceled, and overtime will be mandatory?* She slunk through her office door. *I need to make Leo understand the date is unrealistic.* The phone vibrated again in her hand. She glanced at the message.

—*You forgot to send Kansas with a lunch. Today, we provided a peanut butter sandwich. She also needs a water bottle. We have a drinking fountain but no cups.*—

Mel slid into her chair and sighed at the day care text. She cringed; the future would be late hours and nights at a keyboard instead of spending time with Clay. She tangled her fingers in her hair. Kansas will be the first kid dropped off and the last to go home. *I could quit. I have enough to live on for at least six months, but who would hire me? Besides, I'd be deserting my team.*

"Ring, ring," Paula sang out. "What sound does a bell make? I didn't want to scare you."

She watched Paula saunter into the room wearing a bright-red jumpsuit.

"So, what's up with the big last-minute meeting?

All I know is everyone is hush-hush. Something's up. Spill."

"They're going live with the new software on July fifteenth."

"Boss Lady." Paula shook her head. "The overtime will be crazy. I can't work weekends. We have a new volunteer at the animal shelter, and he's somewhat interested in me."

"Hmm, this sounds promising. Is he tall, dark, and a fantastic puppy poop scooper?"

"Yep, he's a hottie with blond hair and a little short, but you should see how he talks to dogs. He's a pet whisperer, and I hope to get him murmuring in my ear. But if I'm stuck working here, another volunteer will take him home." Paula pouted.

"Did you ever think the volunteer taking him home might teach him a few tricks, and come July, he'll be ready for you?" Mel arched her eyebrows and hoped Paula would agree.

"Clay must not have been looking for a woman with a sense of humor because you're not funny. Hey, why aren't you at lunch with the boys?" Paula hooked her thumb as she emphasized boys.

Mel had the same question but would not voice her concern. *Is Leo up to something? Or am I just paranoid because I'm new to this position and don't understand how everything works?*

"I completely forgot. How did the game go? Did Mr. Tall, Dark, and Handsome make an appearance?"

A fast flutter quickened her heart, and thoughts of the disastrous meeting vanished. Mel let out a soft sigh as she softened her gaze

"Lunch can wait. Spill it, sister." Paula edged

closer.

Mel told her about the proposal.

"Where's the ring?" Paula pointed to Mel's bare finger.

"Opal has missed out on so much these past ten months. I asked Clay to hold the ring until she's back so she can feel included."

"Oh, you're the best sister any girl could ask for. How sweet."

The sudden lurch and twisting in her stomach reminded Mel she was a terrible sister. Breaking promises, causing stress, and instead of protecting Opal, she had caused her pain. *I might have let her down, but I am not disappointing anyone else.* "Why don't you order lunch for everyone? I am hungry for a crispy chicken wrap and fries."

"Got it. I know just the place. The food should be here within an hour. Diet soda?"

"Perfect." Mel turned on her monitor. An email from Leo with the agenda and lunch location. She checked her watch. *No way will I have enough time to get to the restaurant. By the time I walked in, they would have already ordered. Late for the meeting and skipping out on their lunch after the big announcement.* She slapped a palm against her forehead. This isn't good. Leo is probably wondering why he encouraged me to take the management position.

A little after five, Mel received a summons to Leo's office. She had asked Paula to set up a meeting with Leo, but she knew this wasn't at her request. After twenty minutes of listening to Leo dismiss all her suggestions, she stood and started for the door. "It's five-thirty. I need to pick up my niece. I'll review the schedule later tonight and check with the coders' timelines."

Leo rushed in front of Mel and blocked her exit. "Lately, you're not a team player."

Today, Mel didn't cower. She held her ground. "You're the one who asked me to handle Bill's email and remodel project, and I'll only be watching my niece for a couple more months."

"Melody, I didn't ask you here to listen to excuses. What I say stays between you and me." He leaned closer.

As his nose hairs came into view, she stepped back, swallowing hard. *Is he trying to intimidate me?*

"Mr. Hornet is moving the QA, Coding, and Testing Departments to Houston."

She leaned back. "When?"

"August, September latest."

"No one will give up vacations and work eighty-hour weeks when they hear their jobs are moving to Texas."

"You're the manager. You don't ask, you tell." He shook his head. "Besides, there will be jobs available in Houston."

Mel's phone buzzed. "Leo, that's my alarm. I need to pick up my niece." She brushed past Leo and rushed down the hallway to the elevator. She stopped. *I should have asked if any of the positions were in management.* She turned, stepped back toward Leo's office, and spun around. *I don't want to move to Texas. Clay's here. Kansas and Opal are here.*

After slipping into the front seat of her car, she wanted to rest her head on the steering wheel and cry, but she had no time to indulge her emotions. She needed to pick up Kansas and had weeks of work.

When Mel walked through the doors of the day care center, she blinked away a tear.

Kansas sat alone with her backpack as an employee swept the floor.

"Sorry, I'm late, sweetie." Mel braced for a hug, but Kansas didn't run to her.

She stood with her bottom lip quivering.

Mel rushed forward with open arms.

Kansas avoided the embrace, taking four steps before dropping her backpack. "I'm hungry. You forgot to pack my lunch."

The young gal with the broom walked over, picked up the backpack, and offered it to Mel. "You're not the first person to forget to send a lunch. I'm required to say that we might not always have food available. So, if you forget again, we can't promise lunch." The girl leaned closer. "We're obligated to say that, but I'd give up my lunch before letting a kid go hungry."

"I'm sorry, but I forgot your name."

"It's Jillian."

"Jillian, thank you. I want to be you, following corporate policy while having compassion for people. You're epic."

The broom clattered to the floor. Jillian wrapped her arms around Mel. "Thank you."

Mel smiled. Adults needed to be more like young people.

At the door, Mel grasped Kansas' hand. "Come on, let's go home."

"I'm hungry, and I've been waiting a long time." She hugged Mel's legs. "I thought you forgot me." She sobbed.

Mel dropped onto her knees. "I'll never forget you. I had a big meeting, and I had lots of work. Sometimes, work will make me late, but I will never forget you. Let's get dinner. You can choose."

Kansas swiped her wet nose against Mel's shoulder before walking to the car. "Auntie." She pointed. "My jelly bread is on the roof of your car."

Mel laughed. "How hungry are you?"

"Yuk." Kansas stuck out her tongue. "You can eat the jelly. I want chicken fingers."

The evening took a turn for the better. The restaurant had a play center. Kansas ran into friends. They chased each other for over an hour through tunnels, slides, and the ball pit. Mel answered her last email, and at the same time, Kansas rushed back, sweaty with red cheeks. "Come on, kiddo. It's time to go."

At home, Mel gave Kansas a quick bath, tucked her into bed, and within seconds, she saw her niece's closed eyes. She slipped out of her room and down the hall to the kitchen. The microwave numbers glowed nine, zero, zero. *I forgot about calling Clay.* She found her purse and scrambled through the contents to locate her phone. After glancing at the notifications and seeing six missed texts, she wasted no time brushing her thumb across the call symbol.

"Mel?"

"I'm so sorry—hectic day at work. I was late picking up Kansas. She was so hungry and—"

"Take a breath." Clay chuckled. "It's okay. Because if something happened to you or Kansas, you'd call. Right?"

Mel drew her brows together. *Is he questioning me*

because I broke my promise to Opal?

"Up for a late-night snack?"

The wistfulness of his words caused her to chew on her bottom lip. She sighed. "Not tonight. I have a few more hours of work. They pushed up our deadline from November to mid-July. They want all their companies to use a common software program by the first of August."

"If that is unreasonable, couldn't you tell them?"

"You know what Texas' favorite saying is? We don't care how you did things up north. We only care that you do them our way."

"Oh, so you don't have a choice? I could stop by tomorrow with dinner."

"How about this weekend?"

"I'd like to see you and Kansas before then."

"That would be nice, but if I work this week, I should be free on Saturday. Come for breakfast, and stay the day." Mel pictured herself meeting him at the door in her nightgown. "Miss you."

"Miss and love you, too. And don't forget, Kansas has a follow-up with the doctor this week."

"I know. Thanks. Love you and miss you more." She disconnected and opened her laptop. *Can I manage my work and have a life?*

Chapter Fifteen

For the next three weeks, Mel struggled to tackle her workload. She bought extra time from Kansas by giving her whatever she desired. Instead of taking a break on the weekends, she locked herself in her office and delegated parental duties to Clay.

On Saturday mornings, Clay would show up for breakfast.

After a quick kiss, Mel retreated to the office with a pot of coffee. Sometimes, they'd chat for a few moments at lunchtime. Clay would update her on the MN Twinkles as he set a chicken lettuce wrap on her desk and stole a kiss.

"What about getting away for a weekend?" He massaged her neck.

Mel forced her gaze away from the monitor. "Sounds nice. As soon as work lets up." She kissed him. "Any place special?"

"Anywhere, but this office."

The sound of her phone buzzing shifted her attention. She held up an index finger. "One minute." But by the time she ended the conversation with a team member, she discovered the lettuce in her wrap had wilted.

Late one Saturday, she stood to stretch her legs and spotted Clay sprawled on the sofa watching TV. "Hey." She nodded towards her bedroom.

He patted the cushion next to him.

She turned down the lights and joined him. His lips found hers as she snuggled into his embrace, her eyes closed. *Clay?* She squinted at the sunshine pouring through her bedroom window. She lay in bed, fully clothed, with no memory of getting there.

On Sundays, Mel would awake to the insistent ringing of the front doorbell or Kansas chanting, "Uncle Daddy, you're here."

Mel repeatedly thanked Clay for keeping an eye on Kansas. They'd share a couple of quick kisses, and she'd be back in her office.

One Sunday, Mel sat in the kitchen, typing on her laptop when Clay and Kansas walked in carrying a puzzle box.

"Your auntie's fingers peck on the keyboard like a chicken searching for worms."

"Yuk." Kansas scrunched her face.

"Or." Mel continued typing. "Like a woman making everyone at work happy."

"Yuk." Clay scrunched his face and helped Kansas spread the oversized pieces of the kitten puzzle across the table. "Hey, Mel, we might need a little help here."

"Uncle Daddy, these are the kitty's ears, and they go on the top."

Clay studied the furry brown-and-red pieces she held. "How did you know?"

"Not her first time, Clay." Mel laughed. "Before Uncle Daddy, it was Auntie. For eight months, I put the kitties together." She picked up her laptop. "I'll be in my office."

****

On Wednesday afternoon, Mel stared at her

monitors, feeling the pressures of work and life weighing on her. She stretched, trying to ease the tension in her neck and saw Paula stepping into her office. A smile spread across her face. *I've missed her romantic ramblings and teasing.*

Paula shut the door. The steady hum from the printer and the chatter of employees were suddenly muted. She stepped closer. Her gaze focused on the floor.

Mel noticed the paper Paula was holding. "Good news or bad?"

"That all depends. You have a minute?" Paula shifted her weight.

"Not really. Leo hounds me hourly. But for you, I'll make time. What's up?" Mel leaned back and shifted her attention from the stack of papers to Paula's outfit. Today, she wore yellow bell-bottomed pants and a shirt with large orange and green flowers.

Paula cleared her throat. "Boss Lady, what's up are rumors. Lots of gossip flying around about job cuts and relocation. Texas' top dogs have scheduled a roundup on Friday—managers from Information Technology, Coding, QA, and some executives. You need to check those emails. The meeting popped into your calendar an hour ago."

"Rumors move faster than software these days." She clicked her mouse. "Okay, a request just popped into the queue."

Paula shifted and twirled her arms.

Mel watched the flowers on her shirt sway. "You're nervous. You know something."

"First, I love working for you, but this nonsense with the software rollout is swallowing my life. Enough is enough. My weekends should be spent petting homeless dogs, wearing spandex to the gym, and not staring at a computer screen."

Mel slumped low into her chair. "I know. I don't want to spend all my time working. All I do is apologize to Clay and overindulge Kansas. But this crazy overtime and extra work won't be forever. Soon—"

"No. There will be another software upgrade and rollout. Management doesn't care about my life, but I do. What did Tall, Dark, and Handsome say about regrets? Well, you know he's right." Paula slid a sheet of paper across Mel's desk. "I'm giving my notice. Others have considered resigning, too." She dropped her chin. "Can we still be friends?"

The air whooshed from her lungs. She swallowed down words of protest. *They're all deserting me. Worst of all, Paula is leading the way. I've tried to be a good boss, and this is what happens. Besides upper management walking all over me, my employees are trampling over me as they exit.*

"Boss Lady, are you okay? I know this isn't what you want to hear. I'm so sorry."

Mel gazed at her stricken friend. "Hey, don't be sorry." She pushed away from her desk and rushed to wrap Paula in a hug. "I'm just in shock. We'll always be friends. You go get Mr. Puppy Pooper-Scooper."

Paula squeezed her tighter. "I will, and you go get your ring back. Don't let this company squeeze the life out of you."

"I don't know how I'll survive, but I'm happy for you." She stepped back.

"I'll order lunch for the team? I think food would

boost morale."

Mel nodded and tried to smile, but the effort was too much, and she dropped back into her chair and watched Paula step out into the hallway.

I'll miss Paula. Soon, Opal will be home, and she'll take Kansas. The house will be so quiet. My regret won't be that I didn't work longer hours. I'll regret showing Kansas work is more important than family. And Clay, the thought of his quick smile and how he cared for her and Kansas. She blinked at the sudden threat of tears. Closing her eyes, she recalled his scent, the weight of his hand in hers when they walked, and the warmth from his body when she snuggled into the crook of his arm. She tensed. *Accidents happen, people get sick, and there is no guarantee there will be a tomorrow, let alone next year. What if...* She shivered. *In a moment, any of us could be gone.*

She opened a blank document and started her resignation. She dated the letter for the fifteenth of July. *By then, my team will have jobs or a severance package.* She saved the document on her desktop. Before she could compose an apology text for Clay, she heard her cell phone buzz. *Did I forget Kansas' lunch again?* The screen displayed a message received from Clay. Before she opened the text, she felt warmth and longing cloak her like a favorite sweater as she vividly recalled their shared moments. Their first unofficial date at the Twinkles game and the most magical first kiss ever. *Can he sense me thinking about him?* Grinning, she swiped to retrieve the text.

—*Melody, I didn't want to say this in a text. For a month, I tried to get your attention. Lately, we seem to have different desires and goals. I am tired of waiting on the couch every weekend, hoping you'll find time to see me. I want to be part of a team, not the cleanup crew. I guess your heart is more aligned with work than with me. If I'm mistaken, well, then call me.—*

She clenched her fist. *He's dumping me. I thought he understood I needed to be present for my team, and the situation is temporary. If he wanted us to work, we'd have this conversation in person.* She slumped forward and lost her grip on her phone. Ignoring the clatter, she wrapped her arms across her chest, trying to hold the overwhelming rush of emotions from busting loose. *Just when I was going to make everything right, he tosses in the towel. It's like walking out of the game when there is still an inning left to go.*

"Melody!" Leo's voice pierced through the air interrupting her thoughts. "I need that report on my desk by the end of the day. Not first thing in the morning, but tonight, before you leave work."

She peered upward and spotted his bulk looming in the opening to her office. Holding her breath, she dropped her gaze. *The last thing I need is for Leo to see me with a broken heart.* After hearing a loud *humph*, she glanced up and exhaled at her empty doorway. She swiped a tear from her cheek as she re-read Clay's text. *He's not being fair. If he called, I could explain. If you love someone, you don't text. He's a coward.*

"Lunch has arrived," Paula sang, skipping into the office. She slid the lunch across the desk. "You look like death. What's wrong? Is there a problem with Kansas? Opal? What?"

A high-pitched gasp escaped from Mel's gaping mouth.

Paula grabbed the phone with the text still

highlighted. Frown lines creased her forehead as she shook her head. She mouthed the words and gasped. "Call him. Tell him he's wrong."

"It's too late. He'll never believe me now."

"Call him." She raced around the desk and pierced Mel's shoulders with her fingertips. "Tell him it's temporary."

A long-shuddered breath slipped from Mel. "I need to finish a report for Leo. You need to go." She pointed to the door. "Now."

Three hours later, the lunch still sat unopened when Paula shouted, "Come on, Boss Lady. It's five o'clock. Walk out with me."

Mel didn't glance up from her monitor. "Still working. See you tomorrow." She closed her eyes briefly, and her mind filled with conflicting thoughts. *What am I doing at this job? Should I quit? Would my team be better off with someone else leading them?* Five minutes later, she turned off her monitor and snuck down the stairwell like a frightened dog with its tail tucked between its legs. She hesitated halfway down the flight of stairs. *Should I go back?* Sweat beaded up on her brow. *Will Leo force me to resign for not dropping off the report? Will he leverage my inability to manage family and work? No, I can't stay. I have to get Kansas.*

****

Friday morning, Mel hopped out of bed before the alarm. She changed into black slacks and a white no-frill button shirt. She tied her hair back and swiped a bit of mascara on her lashes. Clay had dumped her. Kansas would be gone in a month, and the only thing left in her life would be her job. She'd show them all she could manage.

After dropping Kansas off, she arrived early for the meeting at work. But her confidence faded when she heard the chatter in the conference room echo down the empty hall. *How early do people come to these meetings?* She checked her phone and still had seven minutes before the meeting started. She stepped through the doorway. "Good morning."

The only sound came from the clock on the wall. *Tick-tick-tick.* Then, slowly, one by one, people gave her a slight nod, and she heard a few "hellos" as they began talking amongst themselves. She scanned the room, but no one made eye contact. She'd have Paula check later, but she was sure they had met before she arrived. Feeling like an intruder, she resisted the urge to retreat.

The Texans, positioned at the head of the table, seemed to exist in their own world. Other than a slight tilt of their heads, they carried on as if she were nothing more than a waitstaff, placing menus before them. Their eyes, usually sharp and piercing, now looked dismissive, as if she was yesterday's news.

Did they discuss my flaws, rattling off my mistakes like a prosecuting attorney in a criminal trial? Am I the reason for the palpable tension? Her anxiety mounting, she cast a desperate glance in Leo's direction. Once, he had been her champion, offering her the promotion when others wouldn't have extended her an opportunity. But now he couldn't even look at her, and the weight of uncertainty felt like a heavy stone around her neck.

His gaze dropped to the papers in front of him.

A tight band squeezed her chest, making it hard to

breathe. *Are they firing me? Will they have security guards escort me off the property?* She glanced around the room, and when no one pointed an accusatory finger, she sat on the edge of a chair and strained to listen to the hushed conversations. She inflated her lungs, but the air felt heavy and suffocating. *This could be my last day.* But instead of dread and despair, the constriction in her chest loosened, and she took an easy breath. *Maybe this will be a blessing, and I'll find a job better suited to me.* The glimmer of hope was enough. *I can do this.*

Mr. Hornet, with his cowboy boots and a reputation for being ruthless, walked through the door, and his gaze landed on Mel. "Make yourself comfortable. The meeting shouldn't take too long."

The sound of impatience in his voice caused her to tense. The discomfort increased as he lowered his eyebrows and momentarily sneered. Then, suddenly, his expression brightened as if someone had flipped a light switch, and she witnessed him smiling and nodding at everyone else seated around the table. *Lots of people have it worse, with meaner bosses and challenging jobs.* She swallowed the shame, took a few deep breaths, and tried to ease the pain in her chest.

Mr. Hornet pointed to a calendar on the wall. "The rollout date is now August first. The quality assurance department failed to implement the coding provided by artificial intelligence," he thundered. "Correct me if I'm wrong, Miss Melody. But AI completed the coding on schedule, yet you could not locate the bugs causing said issues."

Mel clenched her hands. "The coding wasn't for the issues we previously identified. We had to rework

168

the testing using the incomplete code."

"Yes. But." He directed his gaze toward Mel. "There will be a successful rollout in August." He placed his palms together, and with both hands held as if they were in prayer, he motioned toward Mel. "In August." He paused. "The first of August. All subsidiaries will be operating on the same software platform. Gascon is the last company to come on board and will go live on August first. After we merge departments and no longer duplicate services."

Mel didn't have to glance around the table to see everyone staring at her because she could feel their glares. When the meeting ended, she gathered her laptop and stepped out the door before anyone else.

The adrenaline from the anger vanished like a caffeine rush from a latte. She slunk into her office and collapsed into her chair. *The rollout didn't fail because of my team's lack of effort but because of the AI coding. The faulty coding increased our time for verification and delayed our ability to discover the bugs.*

She tried to ease the knots in her muscles as she swept her gaze across the desk. *What am I doing here? Is this making me happy? Am I doing the right thing?* She turned on her monitor and sent out a memo. She recapped the meeting but did not confirm or deny rumors of departments merging and job relocating.

I want everyone to have a good weekend. Great job, team. We'll meet on Monday to go over the new timelines.

She leaned back and stretched, but the stabbing pain between her shoulders continued. *I'm not asking my team to do the impossible anymore. No one appreciates their efforts or sacrifices. We all deserve a little breather.* She rubbed the palm of her right hand against her sternum. Tonight, no fast food. Maybe a salad in a quiet restaurant with real silverware and a drink without a lid and a straw. She opened another blank email.

Dear Opal,

The sound of heavy footsteps pounded down the hall. She stopped typing. The last thing she needed was another interruption. Holding her breath, she waited, hoping the steps would echo past her office. The thumping came to an abrupt halt. She glanced over, hovering her fingers above the keyboard.

Leo stood in her doorway.

"Can I help you?"

He sneered and strode to the edge of her desk. "Why would you give your team the weekend off? We need to keep pushing."

Mel slunk back. *Be brave.* She straightened her shoulders and met his gaze. "My team worked night and day for the past four weeks. Instead of a 'good job, well done', they pointed the finger at my team for the delay." She rolled away from the desk. "And what's worse, my team is working themselves out of their jobs, and they don't even know it. Why?" She stood and shook a finger in his direction. "You know why. Because if you tell them their jobs are moving, they'd all quit." The pulse in her temples throbbed as her shaky knees knocked together. "And you don't want them to quit." She leaned over the desk, bracing her trembling arms on the work surface as she snarled. "Why? You know you couldn't hire more competent people who worked harder, or maybe AI isn't perfect. The AI code is incomplete and has led to bugs and errors, but I guess you forgot to tell Texas." She blinked back angry tears.

Leo slammed his hands on her desk, his face inches away as the vein in his forehead pulsated. "Listen, I understand you're under pressure. Others also have families, and all you have is one little kid. It's not that tough. You can manage this." His words sounded strained as he nodded. "You and your team put in extra hours this weekend. And I will see successful tests on my desk early Monday morning."

Mel thought his gaze felt like a dentist's drill, boring a hole through her as her discomfort increased with each passing second.

"Do we finally understand each other?" Leo's question hung in the air as he flashed a big smile.

Mel ignored his attempt at reconciliation or the implied threat and tried to spit out the word, *no*, but her tongue stuck to the roof of her mouth. She watched him walk away. *My team will have the weekend off.* She sat, determined to finish her email.

Dear Opal,

I miss you. This deployment has been challenging for all of us. We all make mistakes. I've made a mess with all my relationships—you, Clay, and work. I am no longer sure which ones can be salvaged. I realize I can't fix things all by myself. I'd like us all to be family, but I will respect your decision if you don't want to or can't.

Stay Safe. Love,

Mel

She inhaled and hit Send without re-reading. Next, she opened the document on her desktop, changed the dates, and sent the letter of resignation to the printer.

My team will be better off without me.

Immediately, the desk phone rang. "Gascon—"

"It's Paula. Leo is at my desk. He wants to know if you sent the revised memo on working this weekend."

"Tell him if he has a question, he should ask me." Mel hung up the phone, stood, and waited.

Leo burst into the room, his voice booming. "I thought I made myself clear. You and your team will work this weekend. Everyone has a lot at stake. Sit back down and inform your team they will be working."

"No." She defiantly crossed her arms before he could see her limbs trembling with a mix of anger and frustration. "Leo, my team has the weekend off. We will meet on Monday and review the new timeline."

He leaned closer. "You misunderstood. This isn't a request."

"No." Mel dug her fingernails into her palms. "My team is not working this weekend. We will meet again on Monday."

"Your team will work this weekend."

Leo's voice was cold and demanding as he strode to the door.

"Send out the memo. Monday. Reports. My desk. I gave you your job, and I can take it away."

Mel listened to his footsteps echo down the hall as she composed the letter to her team, stopping occasionally to rub her sternum. Gasping for breath, she hit Send. Shadows closed in around her eyes. "Paula!"

She skidded through the door and to the desk. "What's wrong?"

Mel clutched her sternum. "My chest feels like it will explode."

"I'm calling an ambulance. You could be having a

heart attack."

She reached for Paula's arm. "I'm not that old. Probably heartburn. Can you drive me to the clinic?"

"No." She swiftly pulled a phone from her pocket. "I think my co-worker is in cardiac arrest." Paula repeated the address, with a tremor in her voice. "Yes, she is conscious and breathing."

Mel sat, listening as the searing pain increased.

"Hey!" Paula rushed to the doorway. "I need someone to go to the lobby, meet the ambulance, and direct them to the fourth floor."

Despite the excruciating pain, Mel stood. "Help me to the lobby."

"You need to wait. We can't risk making it worse." Paula sprinted over and braced a hand on Mel's shoulder while she held her phone with the other.

She brushed her aside. "I'm going downstairs. Grab my phone." She sucked in a jagged breath. "Purse."

"Help, people," Paula barked.

Two men flanked Mel's sides, grasping her arms as she watched Paula rush ahead. Inside the elevator, Mel winced as she struggled to breathe and knew she'd fall to the floor if her co-workers hadn't been holding her. Sweat dripped from her forehead and stung her eyes.

The elevator door creaked open, and they helped Mel into a chair.

"Yes!" Paula shouted, pointing out the window. "Yes, I see the ambulance. They're driving up to the door now."

Mel struggled to fill her lungs as paramedics dressed in black shirts and pants with neon yellow reflective stripes moved her from the chair to a stretcher. She winced. "My chest."

The EMT with red hair and a beard leaned closer. "We'll give you something for pain...a slight prick...these will feel a little cold and sticky...I need your finger..."

She heard the muffled words and struggled to fill her lungs. She huffed, sucking in oxygen.

"Mrs. Anderson, are you allergic to aspirin?"

"No."

"Open your mouth. I need you to chew."

"Paula, phone." Mel could feel her chest heave from the effort of talking.

"Who do I call?" Paula's face contorted. "You never changed your emergency contact. I don't know what to do?"

"Do not call Opal. Call Clay."

"I will, Boss Lady."

Paula's once confident voice sounded forlorn.

The stretcher started moving. "We transmitted your EKG. We're transporting now."

The blinding overhead lights caused Mel to clamp her eyes shut. She cringed.

"...putting an oxygen mask on ...breathe normally...you're doing well. That's it. Deep breaths."

The paramedic's soothing voice calmed her nerves. She could breathe by the time they rolled her into the emergency room. A moment later, she was hoisted off the stretcher and onto a bed. She heard a voice mention another EKG. Mel turned toward the speaker and tried to open her eyes.

"You've had a sedative and will feel sleepy. You're fine."

Each breath came easier as she drifted in and out of

consciousness. Through a haze-induced fog, she recalled arriving at the hospital. The constant beeping and dripping—*where is the noise coming from?* She partially opened her eyes and tried to make out the features in the dimly lit room. *What happened?*

"Hello, Mrs. Anderson. I'm Doctor Carson." The middle-aged man with dark hair and black glasses gave a nod toward a short young man holding a tablet. "And this is my assistant, Theo. I'll need you to answer a few questions."

The doctor rattled off questions about name, address, day, and date as the assistant typed. The doctor smiled. "You're doing great. I just have a couple more. Have you had any traumatic experiences? Death of a loved one, pressure at work, financial issues?"

Mel sharply inhaled at the line of interrogating questions and blurted, "My fiancé broke up with me over a text. My sister's deployed to Kuwait. I'm a caregiver to my six-year-old niece, Kansas. I need to pick her up from day care." She grimaced. "What time is it?" She could feel her pulse increase as she became damp and clammy.

Beeeep. The alarm on the machine screeched.

"Deep breaths." Dr. Carson held her wrist. "In through your nose, good. Out through your mouth. Again. Good." He looked toward the assistant.

"It's a little after seven," the assistant said. "According to the chart, Paula is in the waiting room."

"It's that late. The day care is already closed." Mel could feel anxiety taking hold of her. *What would happen if no one picked up Kansas?* "I need to make sure my niece is okay."

"Does your chest still hurt?"

Mel shook her head. "No. Well, maybe a little ache, but no pain. My heart feels tired. Can I please see my friend?"

"A few more questions and we'll be done. Do you remember when the pain started? Yesterday, this morning, in the afternoon?"

"Today, maybe this morning or it could have been at lunch. Everything kind of blew up. I quit and sent my resignation to—oh no. The letter is on the printer. I need to hand in my resignation. When can I leave?" Mel struggled to get upright. Panic rose in her throat like sour bile. *Paula can help me get Kansas, and then I can go to the office.*

Beeeeeep.

"Breathe." The doctor patted her left arm. "We'll have someone get your friend, and I'll have the nurse bring something to help you relax and sleep. You need to rest so your heart can heal."

"Did I have a heart attack?"

He shook his head. "Heart attacks result from a blockage which restricts blood flow. The stress limited your heart's ability to pump, and your left ventricle temporarily weakened. We can treat your condition with medication. If all goes well, you'll recover within four to eight weeks. We will keep you in the ICU tonight, and if nothing changes, we'll move you to a room on the cardiac floor. Questions?"

Condition. Drugs. I'm too young for heart problems. She flashed back to the weeks after Harold had died from a massive heart attack. She had been in shock and buried herself in work instead of seeing his death as a wake-up call to make changes. "Will I make a full recovery?"

"That depends on your lifestyle choices and your heart. Hopefully, in two to three days, we can release you. We'll send you to a cardiac rehab program. You'll learn stress management and activity modification until your heart heals."

"I need to get home as soon as possible. I don't have anyone to watch Kansas." She shuddered. *What if Paula didn't get a hold of Clay?* "I really need to see my friend and make sure my niece is okay."

"Deep breaths, Mrs. Anderson. If you want to make a full recovery, you need to relax."

"I'm trying." She inhaled and watched the doctor and assistant concur in hushed tones.

The doctor's warm hand gave her wrist a reassuring squeeze. "We'll send your friend in, but only for a few minutes."

As soon as they disappeared, Mel began bargaining with God. *Watch over Kansas, and I'll do better in the future. I'll meditate, eat right, and be more charitable. I'll even learn how to heal my broken heart.*

Chapter Sixteen

Mel knew the sedative was working when she failed to open her eyes at the sound of Paula's voice. *I need to ask about Kansas and Clay.*

"Hey, Boss Lady. The hospital staff told us we could only stay a minute. You need your rest," Paula cooed.

Drifting between sleep and wakefulness, she gave up trying to acknowledge her and lay silently listening.

"Did I do this?"

Mel tensed. *Clay?*

"Not so loud," Paula growled.

His voice stirred up several emotions: regret, longing, pain, and disappointment. She clutched her hands and only grasped the air. *Why can't I wake up?*

"Clay. You broke up with her. Over a text. What type of moron does that?"

"I waited all day for Melody to reply. She never responded."

"You sent a text. You didn't deserve an answer. Real men don't break up in a text." Paula no longer whispered.

"She's busy. Busy with work. I tried—"

"Excuses. Save them for someone who cares."

"You don't understand. I'm a family-first guy. I believed she was family first, too. Did she tell you I proposed?"

"Yes, and she asked you to hang onto the ring so Opal could share in the excitement. That's family first. Taking care of Kansas, family first. Putting loved ones ahead of yourself, family first. Worrying over your employees. Family…first. Whining because someone had to work. Breaking up in a text. Not family first. Know what that is? Me first. That's what I call your behavior, Mr. Tall, Dark, and Dumb."

Warm fingers brush Mel's left hand.

"Melody. Kansas is fine. I'll take care of her until you get home," he stammered.

She swallowed and tried to pry open her eyes as the warmth from his touch disappeared.

"Boss Lady, rest, and don't dream of me or work." Paula chuckled. "I'll swing by tomorrow."

Mel held her breath, listening to machines humming and fading footsteps. *Are they gone?* Loneliness settled over her. *Working without Paula will be hard, but living without Clay?* She shifted her hand to her heart, felt the wires, and blinked back a tear. *And if I lose Kansas and Opal.* She shuddered. *I won't let that happen.*

****

On Saturday morning, Mel moved from the ICU to a room in the cardiac wing of the hospital. She sat attached to the vital monitor, hoping the therapist would soon arrive. She wanted to get back home to Kansas. The door to her room swung open. "Hey, Paula." She tugged her gown into place and tucked her hair behind her ears.

Paula wrestled a gigantic bouquet of balloons through the door. "Hey, Boss Lady. Good to see some color in your cheeks. However, the grayish-blue gown does nothing for your eyes. And your hair, well." She shrugged.

"Good to see you, too." Mel smiled.

"So, they kicked you out of the ICU." Paula set the balloons at the foot of the bed.

"Some of my visitors got a little loud last night."

Paula widened her gaze. "Seriously?"

Mel shook her head and grinned. Teasing Paula felt good after all the drama she'd been through these last few weeks. "I'm doing better, and the doctor expects me to go home on Monday."

"Sheesh. I'm sorry. Guess you heard us talking."

"Thanks for sticking up for me. And insisting I go to the hospital. You saved my life but wrecked Clay's. But hey, he broke up with me in a text."

Paula moved closer to the heart machine. "Yeah, but you could have called him on it. Instead of doing the whole bird with her head in the sand thing."

"I know I should have called out Hornet and Leo, too. So, instead of burying my head, I'm flying the coop." Mel snickered. "Still funny."

Paula moved away from the machine and leaned closer to Mel. "Seriously. You're not funny. But you did a good thing when you sent the memo. Everyone on your team says *thank you*. It's one thing to hear rumors and another to see a letter from your boss about merging departments, jobs relocating to Texas, and incomplete code from AI causing the software testing delays."

Mel sighed. "I hoped Leo wouldn't retract the email."

Leaning closer, Paula shifted her eyebrows lower until her eyes were slits and then tapped her bottom lip with her finger.

"You know drama and withholding information aren't good for my heart. Just tell me already."

Paula grinned as her eyebrows danced like a hula girl's grass skirt. "Oh, he retracted the memo. You should have seen him." She blew out her chest and started high-stepping around the bed. "He huffed around my desk with a red face and wanted to know if there were more memos." She placed her hands on her hips and winked. "Of course, I forgot to tell him to check the printer."

"You found the memo and my resignation and distributed them because you're the best administrative assistant."

Paula grinned. "Yes to the memo. But a *no* to the resignation. I slid your letter into my desk drawer before I left the office. They've scheduled meetings. I'm certain—"

"Thanks, but toss the resignation in Leo's inbox. I quit."

She shook her head. "Boss Lady, maybe you should consider this for a few days. You never know by the time you come back to work—"

"I'm"—Mel poked a finger against her chest to emphasize the words—"not coming back. I quit. The team needs someone to stand up to management." She tensed and shifted her weight. A stabbing sensation behind her sternum had her sucking in a large breath. The machine beeped a little faster. She tried to recall the doctor's instructions, but she couldn't remember if she should suck air through her mouth or nose.

Paula frowned. "Should I call for help?"

"No, I'll be fine." She continued breathing, and the

pain and insistent beeping subsided. "I need to learn to care for myself before I can manage a team."

"You've got this. If you need anything—"

"Thanks." Mel interrupted, no longer wanting to talk about her health. "How's your tail-wagging whisperer? Has his warm breath met your ears?"

"Adorable. He had a fresh haircut and new shorts. He wants to impress someone." She jerked her thumb and pointed at her chest. "We're going for coffee on Sunday morning."

Mel shifted again. "I'm happy for you. Hey, therapy will be here soon. I think I'll rest before they get here."

"Okay. Call if you need anything."

Mel flashed a thumbs-up.

After therapy, Kansas rushed into her room, waving an armful of daisies and baby's breath.

A warmth formed in the pit of her stomach. The first flowers Clay had given her. She searched for Clay and found him hovering in the doorway. Mel waved her left arm. "Clay. Come over here."

Kansas slowly approached the bed, stopping a few feet away. She waved the flowers. "When will you be home?"

Mel extended her hand but could not reach her niece. "They're beautiful and my favorites. Did you smell them?"

Kansas shook her head as her face scrunched. "I forgot."

Clay stooped and held the flowers. "You can smell them now."

Kansas pushed her nose into the bouquet. "Hmm, good." She grinned. "I cleaned my room and put away my toys. Can you come home today?"

"Not today, honey, but hopefully in a couple of days. Come here." She motioned with her hand.

Kansas crawled onto the bed and brushed her fingers against Mel's hospital gown. "How did you break your heart?"

"Too much work and not enough of you." She tickled Kansas.

"You're silly." She frowned. "My mom works all the time. Will she get a broken heart, too?"

Mel held her closer. "No. Sometimes, people get into car accidents, but not everyone who drives crashes. Lots of people work harder than me, but their hearts are fine. Your mom will be fine, and I will be okay, too."

Kansas tapped her chest. "I have a strong heart, too. When you come home, I'll help. You can watch baseball. I'll make a wrap with turkey and lettuce."

Mel staggered kisses across the top of Kansas' head. "Sounds wonderful. I've missed your hugs." Snuggling her closer, she caught sight of Clay biting a nail.

He glanced up and stuffed his hands into his pockets. Clay stepped closer to the bed. "Hey, hi."

"Hey. Hi, yourself. Could you—"

"Yes, yes." His head bobbed. "Whatever you need."

"Clean clothes. Whenever I'm released, I don't want to go home in this beautiful gown. Paula mentioned the gown did nothing for my eyes. I have no idea what happened to my clothes when I arrived. Can I text you a list later?"

"Sure, sure." His eyes glimmered, and he quickly blinked.

Mel hadn't thought about the emotional turmoil Clay had gone through until she glanced into his eyes of unshed tears. She softened her voice. "I'll need a ride home."

"Of course. We'll pick you up and swing by tonight with your clothes."

Kansas hopped down from the bed.

Mel smiled at Clay, hoping she could convey her thoughts. She watched him flash a crooked smile and sighed as she gave a wave.

Mel sent up a silent prayer. *Please, God, let clean underwear be in my drawer and don't let him forget a bra.* The sudden image of Clay wading through her drawer of intimate items had her fanning her face. *I wish I had bought some lacy bikini undergarments. What will he think when he sees a drawer full of ladies' cotton briefs? Ugh! Maybe I should ask him to stop by Sally's Secrets Intimate Apparel for new garments.*

****

On Sunday, Mel smiled and waved at Kansas and Clay as the nurse wheeled her and the balloons to the pickup zone.

Clay rushed to open the passenger door.

Kansas waved from her booster seat window. "Auntie, take the wheelchair, and I'll push you to the park." She pumped her fists back and forth.

"Sorry, kiddo, the wheelchair stays here." Mel took deep, slow breaths, and with help from Clay, she climbed into the front seat.

Clay leaned in close. "So, you're an all-cotton gal."

"I was hoping you wouldn't notice." She smiled. *I hope he still has a thing for the cotton gal.*

****

For the next two weeks, Clay picked Kansas up in the morning and dropped her off in the evening. He rearranged his schedule to drive Mel to all her appointments at the cardiac rehabilitation program, where she met with physical and occupational therapists, a nutritionist, and a counselor. The first couple of days, they glanced awkwardly at each other, but by Saturday, they chatted freely and exchanged lots of smiles.

Thursday of the following week, Mel felt strong enough to attend Clay's softball game. The park showcased six diamonds beside an area for sand volleyball and soccer fields to the far left. They followed the path to diamond four.

The entire team, including Kansas, wore *Construction Dunn Wright* T-shirts with matching caps. Clay nodded toward the players along the first base bench. "Everyone, here are Mel and Kansas."

Mel smiled and acknowledged their waves and greetings with a nod as the team returned to warming up.

Clay walked over and spread a blanket behind the right-side foul line. He set a canvas cooler on the corner. "Bottled water and apples, if you're hungry."

Kansas screwed her face. "No peanuts or candy?"

"Thank you." Mel nudged her niece. "For the beverages and the invite. This is fun. Good luck." She flashed a thumbs-up.

His smile crinkled the skin around his eyes, and he waved. "Okay." He turned and walked toward the other players, stopping halfway. He pivoted and shook his head slightly before covering his grin with his hand and giving an awkward shrug.

A man with a bushy blond mustache rushed over and tugged Clay's shirt. "You need to warm up, not that it will do you much good." He pushed the visor of his cap up and winked.

When the game ended, the first baseman with blond facial hair came jogging over. He stooped into a squat. "I'm Jason. I work with Clay and needed a better look at the lady spinning his head."

"Huh?" Mel twisted and pointed. "You must mean Kansas?"

A deep chuckle split Jason's mouth into a toothy grin. "No, not the little missus." He winked. "You, ma'am. He talks about you all the time. He has it bad. Here he comes. Mum's the word." He winked again and stood.

Clay strode closer. "Whatever Jason says, don't believe him."

"I said nothing but the truth. Clay's a good boss, but he'd be warming the bench if we weren't short players. The guy throws like a girl. No offense to you, ladies." He tipped his hat and walked backward.

Kansas waved. "He's funny. Uncle Daddy, will you teach me to play baseball?"

"Of course. We can go to another MN Twinkles game, and you can catch a foul ball in your mitt." He plopped down on the edge of the blanket.

Mel could feel her chest tightening as she swallowed the lump. She didn't need to see a game to remember the kiss camera or the proposal on the big screen to realize what she had lost. She only needed to glance at Clay. *He could have been mine.*

"Auntie, do you want to catch a ball, too?"

Mel smiled. "Sure, do kiddo. I have a glove in the

garage."

Kansas giggled. "You were a baseball player?"

"No, softball, like Clay. But I played in left field."

"Seriously." He leaned over and gazed into her eyes.

The subtle scent of cedar and citrus teased her senses and sped up her heart, expanding her chest as she inhaled. The grin on her face widened. "Don't be so shocked." She resisted leaning closer and settled for gently poking him in the stomach. "I threw a gal out at home plate more than once."

He leaned back, resting his weight on his left arm as he stretched out his legs. "We'll have to get busy cleaning the garage and find your glove." He arched his right eyebrow, and a slight smile twitched at the corner of his mouth.

Mel shifted her position and scooted closer. "I'd like that." She rested her right palm on his forearm and heard him sigh softly. Heat moved from the pit of her stomach. *Maybe he'll be mine again.*

In week three, rehab gave Mel the okay to drive, but the news didn't thrill her. She shuffled across the parking lot to Clay's truck.

He rushed to open the passenger door.

"Thank you." She climbed unassisted into the cab and waited until he slipped into the driver's seat. "Good news." She forced a smile. "You're done chauffeuring. Rehab says I'm cleared to drive."

He shrugged. "You said good news. I like driving you around."

"Don't get me wrong, I have enjoyed all your services." She hadn't meant to emphasize *all*. Was he also remembering their moments of passion? Flustered, she fanned her face. Trying to move things back to a neutral place, she shifted her gaze to his mouth and then to his hands. "What?" She leaned over and clasped his free hand. "You stopped biting your nails."

His smile turned crooked. "Is that what you were thinking?"

She dropped his wrist. "My first thoughts were of kisses and warm embraces, and then I noticed your fingers." She didn't care if he had flaws. What she cared about was having him in her life. "I guess we both made some changes."

"We have a couple of hours before we pick up Kansas."

She let her gaze linger on his lips. "What did you have in mind?"

"How about a walk?"

"Sure, the weather is gorgeous—and rehab stressed exercising." As he drove, Mel chatted about the end of summer and how September would be here in a few weeks. She clamped her mouth shut. *I'm rambling.*

He pulled into Sunset Park, with its sparkling blue lake, sailboats, and winding bike paths. As she strolled beside Clay, a slight breeze rustled the overhead leaves on the oak and elm trees lining the walk. His fingers brushed against her hand. *No more regrets.* She intertwined her hand with his and tilted her face toward the sun peeking between the branches. "I'll miss this."

Clay suddenly stopped.

Mel skidded to a halt. "What?" She glanced around for impending danger.

Wrinkles appeared between his hairline and eyebrows. "I'm not sure what you're regretting. Saying good-bye to summer? The time away from work? Me?"

The emotion in her heart swelled. She resisted the urge to reach up and soothe his furrowed brow. She gave his right hand a reassuring squeeze. "Come on."

He fell into step, and his grip tightened. "Mel, I don't want to lose you again." He tugged her to a stop. "I am so sorry. I tried to live my life without regrets. But I'll regret sending you that stupid text for the rest of my life."

Mel stiffened, releasing his hand. "I, too, have regrets." She spread her fingers apart before curling her pointer finger. "I regret making a promise I couldn't keep." She bent her middle finger down, trying to keep the tremor from her voice. "I regret not standing up to Mr. Hornet and defending my position and team." She flexed her ring finger tight against her palm. "I regret not quitting on the spot when Leo undermined my care for Kansas." She pulled her pinky in tight to complete a fist. "I regret not calling you after you sent the text. Sometimes, we all have regrets, but regrets are temporary and point us in the directions we need to change."

Clay leaned away from Mel. "What's the fist for?"

Mel shook her clenched right hand. "Break up with me over a text again. This is what you'll get." She gestured and watched the sparkle in his eyes disappear and the smile slide from his face. Gathering her eyebrows in, she covered her face with her hands. "I need to work on my delivery. I want you to fight for me and for us."

He leaned closer and, with a soft touch, uncovered her eyes. "Do you think we could call the first inning of our relationship a rain-out?"

A flutter spread across her stomach, and she

swallowed down the excitement. *Does he want the same thing? Did I misinterpret his words?* "Because we quit too soon or shouldn't have started?" She pressed her knees together to quiet her trembling legs.

He rubbed her upper arms. "Mel..." his voice cracked.

"Are you asking for a makeup game?"

He nodded. "Asking, begging, whatever it takes for another chance."

Drawn into his embrace, she shuddered and tilted her head, sealing the deal with a kiss. *This time, I'll make our relationship a priority.*

****

On Friday, Mel met Paula in front of the Mojo Yoga studio.

"You ready for this, Boss Lady?"

"Not your boss anymore, and rehab says I'm more than ready. Hey, where did you get that mat?"

"Made it. Recycled water bottles and plastic bags."

"I'm impressed. I thought your only talent was ordering lunches." Mel chuckled, walking through the door of the studio.

"Yeah, that and saving my bossy boss' life."

Mel rolled her superstore orange mat out next to Paula. For sixty minutes, they grunted through the beginner class. After their last groans, they rolled up their mats, and Mel swiped the sweat from her brow. "Want to go next door to the Tropical Smoothie Café?"

"Definitely." Paula ripped off her headband and mopped her face as she followed. After studying the chalkboard menu and ordering, Paula leaned her butt against the juice bar. "Boss, you looked good in there. You're all kinds of bendy."

"Three weeks of therapy have paid off." Mel grabbed the drinks and started walking toward a small table in the back. Along the wall stood shelves with an array of potted plants. Some greenery escaped the clay pots and trailed along the walls to the floor. Lazy ceiling fans barely disturbed the hanging beaded curtains. The place had a retro vibe of the 1960s.

"Ow." Paula limped behind. "You'd think I was the one coming out of rehab."

Mel grimaced as customers craned their necks in her direction. "Cardiac rehab."

Paula pulled out an orange metal chair and plopped down at an old wooden round table. "So, the glow. I've seen you with dreamy eyes and a big smile before. Let me guess. Mr. Tall, Dark, and Handsome, or maybe a therapist or a doctor, put the color in your cheeks and the smile on your face."

"Clay." Mel sat on a green chair with a bright sunflower painted on the seat. "We've made up." She took a long sip of her orange surprise. The sudden onset of sour liquid streaming across her tongue pinched her jaw right below her ears. She puckered. "Needs sugar."

"And that's the surprise. It's healthy." Paula drew her brows together. "Is he giving you back the ring?"

The thought of asking him if he still wanted to get married knotted her stomach and tongue. She hoped he wanted to spend the rest of his life with her. "A lot has happened. I'm happy we are back together." She bobbed her head. "I'm hoping he'll talk about the future and long-term plans. Maybe after Opal returns and things are settled, I'll mention it." Flashing a smile, she pushed away thoughts of what if he never asked again?

"Yeah, I guess that might be an awkward subject."

Paula hiked her left eyebrow. "Want me to ask?"

Mel laughed. "I think he's still scared of you. But if you see him again, be nice. He has some single friends. Jason, from his softball team, is cute and funny. Or are you and the doggy whisperer a thing?"

Paula slurped up the last of her purple passion and crushed the cup. "Mr. Doggy Whisperer is no more. It turns out he asks his four-legged friends for relationship advice. That's too weird, even for me. Can you imagine how the man kisses? Bring a napkin, sister."

"Gross. Enough said about him. How's the job hunt?"

"Turns out the Humane Society needed an administrative assistant. The downside is the pay, but they treat me like family. Not like—Oh." Paula widened her eyes, wiggled her eyebrows, and flapped her hands. "I've got news."

Mel leaned forward.

"You'll love this." Paula clapped. "Gascon put the project on hold, and Leo was the only one who relocated to Texas." Paula pumped her right arm like she was blowing the horn on a semi-truck. "Rumor is, Leo wasn't too happy about the move."

"Good. I hope someone suggested Leo buy a cowboy hat." Mel chuckled.

Paula rolled her eyes.

Thirty minutes later, Mel slipped into her car. *It's strange how things work out.* After showering and changing her clothes, she drove into the parents' parking lot at the day care. Stepping from the car, she heard the sounds of children echoing from the playground. At the glass entryway doors, she paused and sighed. Soon, Opal would pick Kansas up. She walked through the doors, smiling and greeting the staff. *I will enjoy these last moments.*

"Auntie. Come on."

Mel braced herself as Kansas came barreling toward her with green-and-yellow paints smeared on her cheeks and shirt and her arms outstretched. At impact, she wrapped her arms around her niece, pulling her tight and kissing the top of her head. "Did you paint today?"

Kansas wiggled free. "How did you know?"

Mel shrugged.

She raised her eyebrows and widened her gaze. "Do you want to see?"

Nodding, Mel allowed herself to be dragged by three of her fingers down the hall and into the art room. She surveyed the table full of painted rocks. "Animals, mosaics, and…?"

"It's a flower." Kansas pointed.

"Beautiful. We can put the stone in the garden at home or save the rock for your mom."

Kansas tapped her right index finger on her chin as her shoulders sagged. "When's my mom coming home?"

Mel smiled. "Four days in Kuwait, seven days at the base in San Antonio, Texas. And then—"

Kansas jumped up and down. "She comes home to me. Let's go, Auntie."

At a little after five, Clay drove up in his work truck.

Some days, they grilled vegetables with chicken or fish; other nights, they made a big salad together.

"How are my girls?" Clay walked through the door with his hands behind his back.

"Uncle Daddy!" Kansas screamed and ran to him.

Like a magician, he produced two bunches of flowers.

Kansas grabbed the bouquets of yellow and white daisies and entered the kitchen. "We're running out of vases."

Mel grinned, because for weeks, he'd been buying flowers. The kitchen, once a place to make meals, now resembled a colorful botanical garden. She slid closer to Clay, wrapping her arms around his waist. "Thank you. I hope this makeup game goes into a lot of extra innings."

"Me, too." Clay brushed kisses across her cheek before lingering on her lips.

Mel closed her eyes. *The only thing missing in my life is Opal.* She took a deep breath. When she got back, there would be time to talk. After numerous sessions with a counselor at the cardiac rehab program, she no longer felt responsible for fixing her sister's problems. She'd always be there to listen, but she didn't have to solve the issues.

Chapter Seventeen

The following Friday, Mel waved the baseball tickets. Her heart raced with anticipation as she jumped joyfully and kissed Clay's cheek. "Guess we won't need to find another vase."

He laughed. "Paula is so wrong about your humor."

"Uncle Daddy. You're home." Kansas rushed through the door.

"Look." Mel held up the tickets. "Seats in left field. We might catch a ball."

"We need to practice. Auntie, if you catch the ball, you can give the baseball to me."

"Kansas." Clay narrowed his gaze. "What if your Uncle Daddy catches the ball?"

She placed her hands on her belly. "Ha, ha. I watched you play softball."

"Well, we all know where you get your sense of humor." He grinned and ruffled her curls.

"How many tickets?" Kansas jumped up and down. "Can I invite Alyssa?"

"Sorry, Shortstop." Clay stooped. "I only have three tickets."

"Okay." She shrugged. "Can we eat? I need to practice catching the ball."

Mel smiled, and joy filled her heart as she recalled her memories at Twinkles' stadium. Now, they'd be making happy memories with Kansas. She tensed. Would there be more events, or would this be the last time she could take her niece? She still hadn't heard from Opal and had no idea if she was still upset.

****

On Saturday afternoon, they eagerly stepped into the MN Twinkles Stadium. "Hurry, Auntie. I don't want to miss batting practice." Kansas pounded her right fist into her glove. "I know I'll catch a ball." She slammed her fist into the pocket again. "Will you take my picture for my mom?"

"Of course," Clay and Mel said simultaneously.

"When's my mom coming home?"

Mel brushed the curls from Kansas' eyes. "Three more days in San Antonio, and then—"

"She'll be home." The slight grin quickly turned into a radiant smile. "Can we take my mom to a game so she can catch a baseball?" She bounced.

"Of course." Mel smiled, too.

"And can we make her a cake and buy presents?"

After wholeheartedly agreeing, Mel positioned Kansas before the Twin City skyline backdrop. She stepped back, leaned against the wall, and exhaled. *What if Clay's wrong and Opal and I can't patch our relationship?* The uncertainty was gnawing, threatening to overshadow the joy of the moment.

"Come on." Kansas yanked on Mel's hand. "We need to get closer to the field." After hustling down the left field stairs, she wiggled next to the other fans who waved their gloves.

The batter connected. *Crack.* The ball sailed into the air.

The young kids raised their gloves as the ball

dropped into left field. In unison, the little ball players sighed and beat their mitts against the rail.

The MN Twinkles players started toward their dugout when left fielder Castro stopped. He called a greeting to the small forest of gloves and picked up a ball from the ground.

"Throw it," the kids pleaded.

He grinned and tossed the baseball into the stands. After the fourth toss, he waved to the crowd again.

Kansas checked her mitt. "Missed again. Next time, I'll be ready," she shouted and punched her fist into the pocket of her glove.

Castro picked up one more ball and walked toward Kansas. "I think you're ready now." He tossed the ball up into the air.

Kansas held her glove up high and squinted her eyes shut.

A boy with red-and-blue spiked hair had his glove poised for the catch. Sure enough, the ball dropped into his open glove. But instead of closing his grip, he dropped the ball into Kansas' glove before she opened her eyes.

The crowd cheered.

Kansas peered into her glove, her face beaming with joy and pride. She raised the ball. "Look. Look. I caught it. I caught the ball."

The crowd stomped their feet on the deck.

The Baltimore Os took the field next for batting practice.

But after forty-five minutes, Kansas lost interest. "I don't need another baseball."

They climbed up the stairs to their assigned seats as more fans, carrying trays of drinks, nachos, and cotton candy, entered the arena.

"I'm hungry." Kansas pointed to the fans shuffling past with treats.

Clay brushed the curls from her eyes. "When the game starts, food vendors will bring fresh peanuts, warm hot dogs, and ice-cold sodas. Or we can walk through the long crowds to the concourse." He slowly walked his fingers along Kansas' armrest.

"Hmm." Kansas tapped a finger on her bottom lip.

A stadium attendant stopped at the end of the row. He leaned toward Kansas. "Did you catch a ball today?"

"Yeah, in my glove." She pushed her right hand into the mitt pocket and removed the ball. "Does he want it back?"

"No, that's your ball, now. MN Twinkle Dog is looking for someone with a glove who can catch."

"I can catch." Kansas danced in front of her seat. "I'm a big helper, too. Can I go? Please, Auntie? Please, Uncle Daddy?"

Mel glanced over at Clay and watched him nod.

The usher stood. "Okay, folks, follow me."

Kansas fell in step behind the man.

Clay grasped Mel's hand.

She smiled. The path wound through the stadium, before going down seven steps. As she stepped through a doorway, the concrete walls blocked the sound of the excited fans. The hallway was cooler and artificially lit, and before long, she reappeared at the north ramp. Mel squinted as she stepped into the sun. She squeezed Clay's hand. "Is she going onto the field?"

The usher turned. "Yes, but we'll have you two stand off to the side where you can take pictures. MN

Twinkle Dog will meet her by home plate."

Clay pointed to the big screen where the costumed dog appeared larger than life.

"Today." The announcer's voice boomed through the microphone. "We have a very special assistant to help MN Twinkle Dog at home plate. Let's give a big round of applause to welcome home from Kuwait, Army Captain, Opal Erickson. And to help her catch the first ball of the game, we have Captain Erickson's daughter, Kansas."

Opal stepped out from behind the mascot.

Mel gasped and slid her right hand over her chest as tears glistened. "She's home." Pride gleamed from her eyes as she stared at her sister dressed in her uniform, cap, and boots.

"Momma, Momma, Momma," Kansas screamed, crashing into outstretched arms.

Raining kisses on Kansas' cheeks, Opal twirled around, and with each revolution, her smile widened.

"USA. USA. USA," the crowd chanted.

The announcer's voice vibrated above the crowd. "Looks like Twinkie is ready to start the game."

Opal settled her daughter in front of home plate. She pointed toward the pitcher's mound.

Kansas nodded and held open her baseball glove

MN Twinkle Dog tossed a ball.

Smack. The baseball landed inside the pocket.

The crowd cheered.

Mel sighed. *Opal's home.* She expanded her lungs, drawing in an easy breath after months of worry. Feeling like she could float away, she turned to Clay. "How? What?"

He held his phone focused on the field, smiling and

nodding as he continued recording.

Opal and Kansas rushed into the corridor and wrapped their arms around Mel.

She clutched Opal. "I can't believe you're here and in one adorable piece," Mel squeaked, as the words passed the tears in her throat. "I missed you." When they started back up the ramp, Mel caught a glance between Opal and Clay. *Did he help her set this up?*

"Mommy, you're home."

Opal scooped her up. "I know, baby. Look how much you've grown." She ran her fingers through her thick curls. "You can ride a bike and catch a baseball. I'm not sure what's left to teach you."

"I still don't know how to drive a car." Kansas buried her face into Opal's uniform. "My happiest day."

For the game's first three innings, Kansas sat in Opal's lap.

Mel continued to shift her gaze between her sister and Clay. "I can't believe she's home." She rested her head on his shoulder. "I still can't believe this is happening. At an MN Twinkles game, no less."

He wrapped an arm around her shoulder and pulled her closer. "Good thing you like baseball."

The emotion in his voice tugged at her heart. She snuggled closer, bumping into the armrest. Thoughts of their first kiss and being thwarted by seats brought back the passion. Heat seared her cheeks, and she squelched the desire to kiss him again. At this stadium, he proposed and now a homecoming. She rested a hand over the flutter in her chest. Happiness, love, and a sense of being whole expanded her chest, and the burden of worries about the future vanished. She wrapped her fingers around his bicep. "It's a little odd, but I think we might need to buy season tickets." Mel wiped her eyes dry again. "I love a good game and you." At the top of the fifth inning, Mel nudged Opal. "Okay, how did you come up with this surprise?"

Opal grinned and pointed a finger at Clay. "He set the whole thing up, and I kept quiet. Which wasn't easy to do. So many times, I wanted to tell you. But the look on Kansas' face was worth every aching moment." She winked and lightly jabbed Mel. "Your face was precious, too." She chuckled.

After the seventh inning, vendors traveled the stairs as they shouted, "Sailor Jack, get your caramel sailor box popcorn."

Clay purchased four boxes.

Kansas eagerly tore into one box. "I'm finding the prize." After digging for a moment, she raised her right hand and waved her sticky caramel popcorn fingers. Her fist looked like a creepy alien's hand. She tore the paper wrapper apart. "I have a sticker."

Opal leaned over. "Kansas, you have a tattoo. You next, Mel."

Mel shrugged, opened her box, and plucked the prize from inside. She didn't have to open the wrapper to know she had a ring. Tears brimmed in her eyes as she opened the paper to reveal a familiar pearl and diamond ring. "Oh, Clay. Your grandmother's ring." She held the ring out. "My hands are shaking. Clay." She blinked. "Oh, Clay."

He slid the ring on with a steady hand. "It's your ring now. I love you." He kissed her.

Mel could feel her heart thumping against her chest as she held him tighter. She blinked away her tears of joy. "I love you, too."

"Auntie, your ring was in the box. Mommy, you next." She clapped her hands. "Maybe you have a ring, too."

Opal drew out her prize and opened it. "I have a tattoo just like you, Kansas. Let's put them on our forearms. Peel back the paper, hold tight, and count to ten."

"Ten." Kansas squinted at her right forearm. "This doesn't make any sense."

"Let Auntie see."

Mel looked at their arms. More tears rolled down her cheeks. "Flower Girl. Maid of Honor."

Opal leaned into Mel. "I know you haven't asked, but I'd like nothing more than to help you celebrate your big day. Clay, you don't have to open your box. I had two prizes in mine."

He took the prize Opal held out. "I have a tattoo, too." Moments later, he peeled back the paper and flashed his tattoo. *World's Best Daddy.*

Mel reached over and brushed the curls from Kansas' eyes. "You're right, sweetie. Best day ever."

Opal backhanded the tears from her eyes. "The very best. Thank you both. I'm so happy we're all family."

Mel smiled. *The only thing left to do is show Paula my ring for this to be the ending of my happily-ever-after love story.*

Chapter Eighteen

A month later, Mel brushed her hands against the white lace of her dress as the sun glistened off Clay's fresh-cut lawn. A ribbon of tiny white lights beckoned guests from the front walkway to the backyard. On the center stage stood a timber-framed wedding arch adorned with more lights, daisies, and clusters of baby's breath. Mel stood next to Opal in the enclosed porch and watched the preparations.

Clay carried two more folding chairs to the front row and set them down. He hugged his parents and then motioned them into the chairs.

Opal nudged Mel. "I'm not sure you'll have enough chairs; there might only be standing room. You ready for this?"

"More than ready." Mel fanned her eyes. "You have lots of tissues?"

"When can I go?" Kansas held out her baseball mitt stuffed with flower petals.

"In a minute, honey." Mel straightened her veil and scooped her wedding gown train.

"Remember, Kansas." Opal held the baseball glove shut. "You take a step, sprinkle a few petals, another step, more petals. Just like we practiced."

"I know, I know. Auntie, you're beautiful. Mommy, you're beautiful, too. But Auntie's the princess today."

The door flew open, and Paula stepped through. "Wow, look at you gorgeous ladies. I just wanted you to know Mr. Tall, Dark, and Almost Married said, 'Whenever you're ready.' "

Mel held out her arms. "Paula, thanks again. From best admin to best wedding planner. I don't know what I'd do without you."

Paula stepped into Mel's embrace. "Does this mean I can start the show?"

"Start the show."

"Sure thing, Boss Lady." Paula danced out the door.

After the first note played, Kansas shot through the door and ran halfway to the wedding arch before stopping. She opened her glove and set a couple of petals down, shuffled an inch, dropped a few more petals, waved, and a few more flower petals hit the ground.

Opal motioned for Mel to come closer.

She peered through the opening at her niece.

"I hope you're not in a rush to get married. It looks like my kid is taking her time."

Mel swept her gaze over the yard and drew in a big breath. The flower petals her niece dropped look so vibrant and the sky a brighter blue. A feeling of being invincible flooded through her. Being in love with Clay expanded all the good things in her life. "Pinch me. Is this real? You home, me marrying Clay. I feel like I'm dreaming."

"Not a dream. I love you, and I am happy for you." Opal wrapped her arms around her.

"I'm done." Kansas screeched. "Hurry, Momma. Everyone wants to see Auntie."

"I guess that's my cue." She started for the door. "See ya out there, sis."

Mel tried to steady her shaking hands as she fumbled, opening the door. Standing in the middle of the yard was Clay in his tuxedo. He stood looking at her with nothing but love. She resisted the urge to run into his arms. As she promenaded past the rows of chairs, she registered a flutter starting in her stomach and moving to her heart. She had never enjoyed being the center of attention, but today, she was thrilled to have everyone present to see her wed Clay. She had never felt more love.

He held out a hand.

She interlocked her fingers with his and leaned into her husband-to-be. "Happiest day—"

"Ever," Clay finished.

After exchanging vows and the rings, she couldn't pull her gaze from his eyes. *My husband.* She moistened her lips as she leaned in and gently placed her left hand behind Clay's head. The warmth of his palm barely brushed against her right cheek. She rested her right hand on his elbow as the heat from his touch warmed her waist. Slowly, she moved her lips forward to meet his, the touch tentative, at first. She closed her eyes, and everything else faded away until there was only Clay. The pressure increased as their breaths mingled, and a rush of feelings washed over her and she couldn't resist taking a peek. *Did he feel the electricity mixed with euphoria?* One look into the sparkling brilliance of his chocolate diamond eyes confirmed he was experiencing similar emotions. She melted into his embrace as the kiss ended. The thrill of their first kiss on the big screen was nothing compared to the rush of emotions radiating through her.

"Let me introduce…" the preacher shouted. "Mr. and Mrs. Westby."

The kiss ended as the clapping erupted, but the feelings of love only increased.

They started down the aisle, as guests tossed peanuts and popcorn into the air.

"Ow." Clay ducked. "I tried to tell Paula peanuts were a bad idea."

Mel laughed. "That's okay. When she gets married, we will toss bags of dog doo-doo."

"I heard you, Boss Lady. And you're still not funny," Paula shouted. "This is the thanks I get, folks, for bringing this happy couple together."

Later, Mel watched Clay's parents beam as Kansas tugged on their hands. "Come, Grandma and Grandpapa, I want you to meet my friend, Alyssa."

The rest of the day flew by. So many friends wanted to wish them well in their new lives together. As she waved good-bye to the last guest, Mel turned to Clay. "I've never been happier. My cheeks hurt from smiling, but I can't stop grinning."

He hiked his right eyebrow higher. His tongue moistened his lips. "Best, happiest day ever. Want to work on the best night?"

"Yes, I do." She closed her eyes as his lips found hers. *I can't imagine ever being happier than I am at this moment. I am so glad I took a chance.*

****

Four months later, snow fell on what used to be Mel's driveway. The light dusting of white complimented the red-and-green Christmas lights twinkling along the garage roof. She felt Clay's gloved hand brush against her mitten and clasped his hand. "Look." She pointed to the glowing luminaria candles along the walkway to the front door. "Oh." She gestured to the snowmen, penguins, and giant candy canes vying for top billing in the front yard. Santa and his reindeer lit up the roof. On the door, a pine-scented wreath hung.

Clay released her hand and adjusted the packages he was carrying. "The only thing missing is mistletoe."

Mel smiled. "I'm sure it's here somewhere." She brushed her lips over his as her hip hit the doorbell.

The front door opened. "Welcome," Opal sang out. "Merry Christmas." She ushered them inside.

Mel stepped into the house, hugging her. "The yard is magical. I can't believe this is my old house. You've been busy."

She stepped back. "Thanks. You don't think it's too much?"

"Not at all." Clay leaned around Mel to greet Opal. "Merry Christmas."

Kansas held her arms out like a programmed robot. "Coats." She staggered from the weight of the jackets. "I'm the best helper. I've been good all year. Santa's bringing me ice skates and a hockey stick. Alyssa plays hockey, and I want to play, too. Wait, I'll be right back." She trotted down the hall.

Mel motioned for her sister to come closer. "What happened to wanting a skateboard?"

She shook her head and rolled her eyes. "Santa has been buying and returning things all week long."

"Ho, ho, ho. Anybody home?" a woman's loud voice penetrated the door.

Kansas rushed back, huffing. "Who's at the door

now?"

"I hope someone's home," a man shouted. "Because I'm freezing my jingle—"

"Sounds like elves or Paula and Jason." Mel swung the door open.

"Expecting someone else, Boss Lady?" Paula rushed in with her arms full. "We bring wishes for a Merry Christmas."

"And…" Jason grinned. "We might have a few gifts for the little one." He winked at Kansas. "Your daddy says you've been good."

"I have." Kansas stretched her arms out. "See, I'm taking your coats."

After a traditional Christmas dinner, they moved into the living room, patting their full stomachs.

"Cookies?" Paula asked.

Everyone groaned as they found a place to sit around the tree.

Opal flipped a switch, and children's Christmas music drifted from speakers. The tree lights started flashing and blinking as if dancing to the beat.

Lots of "oohing" and "aahing" sounded from the guests.

Mel reached under the tree and pulled out a large red-and-white tote bag. "I know Santa doesn't come until tomorrow, but we have a few gifts we'd like to share."

Kansas clapped and danced around. "Presents. Do you have one for me?"

Clay handed a wrapped box to Kansas and one to Opal.

Kansas ripped at the wrapping paper, and the lid flew across the floor. She busted through the tissue paper and waved a red hooded sweatshirt high into the air like a cheerleader. "It says something." She traced the letters on the sweatshirt as she sounded out the words. "I am the big sister." She shook her head. "I am the big sister." She shrugged.

"Oh, oh." Opal's gaze widened as her gaze shifted between them. With shaky fingers, she ripped at her box.

Clay handed a box to Paula and one to Jason.

Opal popped out of her chair, waving her hoodie. "I'm an auntie." She tossed her arms around Mel. "When? How do you feel? I can't believe you didn't tell me."

Paula danced. "A godmother."

Jason clapped Clay on the back. "Don't worry, man. I'll teach the kid to play ball. I'll be the best godfather."

"What?" Kansas shouted. "What's going on?"

Opal swooped Kansas into her arms and spun her around, bumping into Paula. "Your daddy and auntie are having a baby sister."

"Huh?" Mel waved her hands and cocked an eyebrow in Clay's direction. Did they use the wrong color lettering on the shirts?

Opal set Kansas down. "I'm confused." She shook her head. "Is there going to be a baby?"

"Yes, we're pregnant, but we're having a boy. Kansas, you'll have a brother."

"A baby?" Kansas tilted her head. "A brother." She clapped. "Best day ever."

Mel smiled. "Yes, this is the best day ever, and it all started with a chance meeting."

A word about the author...

I believe you should fall in love as many times as possible...even if it is with the same person...and you should laugh.

I took a ten-year break from writing to travel, explore, and volunteer, and have come back to one of my first loves, writing.

I have been published in fiction romance, creative non-fiction, poetry, and children's fiction

ChristineColumbus.net